# Inside Grandad

# Inside Grandad

## Peter Dickinson

WENDY
LAMB
BOOKS

Published by Wendy Lamb Books
an imprint of
Random House Children's Books
a division of Random House, Inc.
New York

Visit us on the Web! www.randomhouse.com/kids
Educators and librarians, for a variety of teaching tools, visit us at
www.randomhouse.com/teachers

Library of Congress Cataloging-in-Publication Data
Dickinson, Peter, 1927–
Inside Grandad / Peter Dickinson.
p.   cm.
Summary: Gavin tries to enlist the help of selkies—seal people—to communicate with his
comatose grandfather.
ISBN 0-385-74641-5 (trade) — ISBN 0-385-90873-3 (library binding)
[1. Grandfathers—Fiction.   2. Coma—Fiction.   3. Selkies—Fiction.
4. Scotland—Fiction.]   I. Title.
PZ7.D562In 2004
[Fic]—dc21                                                                     2003007862

Printed in the United States of America

February 2004

10 9 8 7 6 5 4 3 2 1

BVG

*For all at Maisley, including Shaggy*

# 1

Gavin and Grandad were fishing for mackerel from the harbor wall when the seal popped its head out of the water. For a moment Gavin thought it was a loose net-float bobbing about. Then he saw the two eyes, large, round, and glistening black, staring straight at him. The thing rose a bit more and he saw the whiskery muzzle and knew what he was looking at.

He'd never seen a seal that close. They often came to Stonehaven but usually stayed farther out. What's more, though it must have seen Gavin, it didn't duck out of sight but stayed where it was, staring. Gavin stared straight back.

"It looks like Dodgem begging for handouts," he said.

(Dodgem was Gran's dog, a sort-of-bulldog. He looked tough, but was really a total wimp, and lazy and greedy with it. You couldn't imagine him dodging anything. Gavin's elder brother, Donald, swore he'd once seen him collide with an old woman with a walker, though he'd been moving slower than she had. Grandad and Gavin didn't pay much attention to him. He was just there.)

Grandad hadn't seen the seal because he was putting his tackle away. The harbor wasn't the best place to fish, but there wasn't time to go anywhere else between Gavin coming out of school and getting home to cook tea. Still, they'd been lucky that afternoon. Gavin had hooked into a half-size mackerel almost at once. Perhaps he should have thrown it back, but he'd kept it because they mightn't get anything else, and by the time they'd caught five more good ones it was dead.

Now Grandad looked up, grunted, and picked the half-size fish out of his creel. Gavin took it and tossed it to the seal.

The seal wasn't a trained seal in an aquarium, so it didn't reach up and catch the fish in midair but snapped it up just as it hit the water, and dived out of sight.

Tacky Steward, fishing twenty yards off along the wall, shouted at Grandad for encouraging seals to come to the harbor. They scared the fish off, he said.

"Plenty to go round," said Grandad mildly. Nothing fazed Grandad. That made Tacky even madder. He hadn't caught much. He never did, and it was always someone else's fault. He shouted some more and the seal popped its head out of the water as if it wanted to see what the fuss was about. The mackerel's tail was sticking out of the corner of its mouth until the seal threw its head back and sort of gargled it down.

"You're welcome," said Gavin.

The seal blinked, as if it hadn't expected to be spoken to like that.

"See you soon," said Gavin. The seal seemed to nod before it dived out of sight.

"Mr. Steward's right, though, isn't he?" Gavin said as they trudged up the hill. "If you feed the seals they'll come for more."

"Maybe," said Grandad. "But Tacky's got no cause to go yelling at me like that. There's ways of making your point, and ways of not."

"I liked the seal," said Gavin. "It looked like it knew what I was saying to it."

"Could be," said Grandad.

"What do you mean?"

"There's more to seals than they show you on the telly. Know what a selkie is, boy?"

"A selkie?"

"They're seal-people, selkies. See them in the water, and they're seals all right. But come ashore, and you wouldn't know them from people. There's stories of selkie women falling in love with farmers, and marrying them, and living on land for a while and raising a family, until the pull of the sea got too strong for them and they went back and turned themselves into seals again."

"You don't really believe that."

"Tacky doesn't. No imagination."

You didn't always get a straight answer out of Grandad. Gavin tried somewhere else.

"Did they have children—the selkie women who married the farmers?"

"Says so in the stories."

"Some of them would have been selkies too, wouldn't they? Half selkies, anyway?"

"Stands to reason."

"Do you think we've had any of them in our family? We can't keep away from the sea either."

(Far back as anybody knew, the Robinson men had always been sailors, fishermen or seamen on merchant ships, mostly.

3

Grandad had been a ship's engineer. Dad was first mate on a big container ship. He was in the Caribbean right now. Donald was in Edinburgh, training to be a doctor, but chances were he'd finish up doctoring people on a ship.)

"Don't see why not," said Grandad.

They fell silent and trudged on up the hill to Arduthie Road. Stonehaven was a steep, dark gray town nestling round its bay. It was always uphill going home.

Grandad was the most important person in Gavin's life. Once, when Gavin was smaller, his teacher had told her class to draw their mums, or whoever else looked after them. Gavin had drawn Grandad. It was a small kid's picture, of course, all wrong, but you could still see it was Grandad, short and square, with a shiny bald head, brown and mottled, and with spectacles and a bushy gray mustache. In Gavin's picture the mustache was almost as big as Grandad's head.

Gavin had a perfectly good mum, and she lived in the same house. So did Gran, and Dad too, when he was home, but most of the time he wasn't, and Mum and Gran both worked. Mum was an estate agent, helping people buy and sell houses, and Gran sold things at Hankin's, the big hardware store down in the square. Grandad was eighteen years older than Gran, so he'd retired when Gavin had still been small, and soon after that the family had sold their two separate houses and bought the one in Arduthie Road. The idea was that Gran would look after Gavin so that Mum could go back to her job, because they needed the extra money; but almost at once Gran had got bored with that arrangement—she needed people to talk to, even if it was only about size-ten countersunk screws and stuff—so she went back to work too and Grandad started doing the looking after.

So it had been Grandad who'd taken Gavin to his first school and fetched him back and done things with him after and cooked his tea and put him to bed like as not, because Mum often worked late, showing houses to clients, while Gran cooked grown-up tea. Nowadays, when Gavin didn't go to bed much earlier than anyone else, he and Grandad cooked what Grandad still called tea and Mum called supper. Sometimes Gavin wondered a bit guiltily if it would make a lot of difference if Mum and Gran just vanished one day and never came back. Not much, he decided, except that the house would be a lot quieter in the times when they used to be there. (Gran liked to talk. She did it like breathing—all the time. Mum wasn't so bad, unless there were plans and arrangements to be made. She could out-talk Gran then, no problem.)

But if Grandad vanished . . . He was seventy-four already. . . . He was bound to die one day. . . . Gavin couldn't bear to think about it.

The great thing about Grandad was that he understood what it was like being Gavin. He always had, even when Gavin was small—understood what made him miserable or happy or angry or afraid, even things that Gavin was ashamed to talk about to anyone. Like when Dave Murray had been giving him a hard time in his fourth year and he didn't want anyone to know how scared he was of going to school each morning, but Grandad had noticed and got it out of him and told him how to deal with it. He'd let Gavin think he'd done it all on his own too, but later on Gavin guessed that he'd gone round and seen Mrs. Whebbery after school and sorted it out with her.

They had the mackerel for tea. Gavin split and filleted them and brushed them with egg and then rolled them in oatmeal, while Grandad peeled the spuds and put them to steam and sliced the beans. It was his turn for the boring jobs, except that he got to make the mustard-and-onion sauce. When the pinger went Gavin fried the mackerel while Grandad put the beans to steam and set the table. That way everything was ready, as good as it could be got, all at exactly half past six— except that Mum was still out selling a house and Gran was on the phone to Sissie Frazer, and good for another half hour at least. That meant Gavin and Grandad could have their tea in peace and quiet. Grandad read his *Model Boats* and Gavin did the reading part of his homework.

"What does 'punctilious' mean?" he asked at one point.

Grandad reached back and took the dictionary off the window-sill and passed it across.

"Thanks," said Gavin.

Those were the only words they spoke all through the meal. Dodgem made up for their silence by whimpering with anxiety, and from time to time heaving himself out of his basket and plodding off to the hall to check if Gran was anything like finished on the telephone. He got to lick her plate when she'd eaten.

# 2

Next day was Saturday, and wet. Gavin was in Grandad's room at the top of the house, getting his homework finished so as to free up the rest of the weekend. Grandad was working on his boat. He built the most beautiful model boats, better than anything Gavin had ever seen in a shop. They weren't just models to stand on a shelf. You could set their self-steering gear and put them in the water and they'd sail themselves, or you could control them by radio.

This one was a trawler, of the kind Grandad's own grand-father had worked on until he'd been drowned in a North Sea storm. You could see she was an old boat, which had fished in all weathers and brought her catch home to harbor again and again and again. Her paint was fresh, but she had a used and battered look and a patched rusty-red sail, and the coils of rope and piles of net on her deck were pale gray with soaking in salt water and drying out in the sun—Grandad had experimented for weeks, soaking cord in different mixtures to get them right. It usually took Grandad several months to build a boat. People ordered them from him and paid thousands of pounds for them, and even then they'd have to wait a year or two before they got theirs.

But this one was for Gavin, for his eleventh birthday next month. It was almost finished.

"Couple more days should do it," said Grandad as he started to clean his brushes. "Another coat on the wheelhouse and a bit of filling and touching up on the stand. Thought of a name for her yet, boy?"

Gavin had been worrying about this almost since Grandad had started. None of the names he'd dreamed up had seemed quite right. Now a new one seemed to leap off his tongue without his having to think at all.

"*Selkie*," he said.

"Good enough," said Grandad. "No harm in having the selkies on your side—they'll give you a hand if you're in trouble. But they can be touchy too, if the stories have them right. You'd best go down to the bay and ask them if they mind."

He twisted his chair round and started to stand up. That was when it happened. His whole body gave a violent jerk. His left arm flailed out, knocking his jar of brushes over and spilling painty turpentine across his workbench. His face twisted, with his mouth wide open and pulled sideways as if he were trying to scream, but all that came out was a ghastly croaking sound. He jerked again and fell forward. Gavin rushed to catch him, but he was knocked aside and Grandad hit the floor with a thud that shook the house.

Gavin was half winded but he forced himself to his knees beside Grandad's body.

"Grandad! Grandad!" he croaked, and shook him by the shoulder.

The shoulder felt wrong. The arm flopped about. The other arm was jerking around, the hand grabbing at empty air. Grandad's face seemed lopsided. His blue eyes were wide open, staring. There was a horrible rasp in his breathing, with a gulping sound between breaths. Gavin called again, twice, and then raced down the stairs to the hall. He realized Grandad had had a heart attack or something, and knew from the telly that there was no time to lose. He picked up the phone and dialed 999. A man answered second ring.

"Emergency services. How can we help?"

"I think my grandfather's had a heart attack. He's fallen down and he can't hear me. There's no one else in the house."

"Hold the line. I'll put you through."

A woman this time. He gave the same message, then the address and telephone number. She told him to hold the line and some music came on. He thought of something else while he was waiting. The woman came back.

"The ambulance is on its way from the Kincardine Hospital," she said. "It shouldn't be more than ten minutes. Will you be ready to let them in?"

"Okay," he said. "Can you tell them he's at the top of the house? The stairs are pretty steep."

"They'll manage," she said. "Don't worry. He'll be all right."

Gavin's hands started to shake as soon as he rang off but he managed to call Mum's mobile. She couldn't answer while she was with a client, so he left a message. He tried to call Gran at Hankin's, but they were engaged. He couldn't bear to be away from Grandad much longer—what would happen if he suddenly came round?—so he propped the front door open with a wellie and scrawled a note on the telephone pad saying "Ambulance men. Come right upstairs" and put it on the doormat. He didn't know if he'd spelled "ambulance" right, but it didn't matter. He tried Hankin's again, but they were still engaged so he raced back up.

Grandad was lying as Gavin had left him. He was still breathing with the same horrible rasp and gulp. His face was blotchy.

Gavin didn't dare move him, so he covered him with the old rug Grandad used to wrap round his legs when he was working on a boat in the winter. His spectacles had come off in the fall and were lying beside him, so Gavin picked them up and put them in his own shirt pocket. Grandad's right hand had got hold of the edge of the rug and was twitching it about as if it was worrying him. Gavin eased the rug away and put his hand into Grandad's and held it, winding their fingers together. He'd expected the hand to feel different, strange, half dead, but it was firm and warm, with rough places on the palm. Grandad's hand, except for the way it fidgeted about. But alive.

And the woman had said he'd be all right. Of course, she had to say that. She couldn't know.

"You'll be all right, Grandad," he croaked. "You'll be all right."

A man's voice shouted, down below.

"Up here," Gavin called.

Feet thumped on the stairs. Two men came hurrying in with a folding stretcher. The one behind was Garry Toller's dad. When he wasn't on duty, he sometimes came down to the Leisure Center to referee the football. He knew Grandad.

Gavin started to get up.

"No, stay where you are for the mo," said the first man. "You're doing no harm."

He knelt and pulled the rug aside.

10

"Old Robbie Robinson!" said Mr. Toller, recognizing him now. "And young Gavin, of course. Where's your mam, Gavin?"

"Working. I've left a message on her mobile. Gran's working too, but they're engaged."

"Why don't you go and have another try while we're getting your grampa down the stairs," said the other man. "It'll take a wee while. Places some people choose."

He started to unroll the stretcher. The other man was getting something out of his pack. It looked like an oxygen mask.

"If I get her shall I tell her to come to the Kincardine?" said Gavin. "Is that where you're going?"

"First off, so the doctors can take a look at him," said Mr. Toller. "But they'll be sending him on to the Royal Vic, if I know anything. Or maybe Perth. Off you go now."

Gavin hurried down the stairs. The Royal Vic was the big hospital in Aberdeen. He hoped they didn't take Grandad there. It was too far to get to every day. Perth was even farther. The Kincardine was actually in Arduthie Road, right up at the other end, but still only ten minutes' walk.

The telephone rang and rang. The ambulance men had done the difficult bit from the attic and were starting down the main stairs before a man answered. Gavin started to give him a message for Gran.

"Hold it," said the man. "I'll get her."

"No, wait!" said Gavin desperately. He didn't want to talk to Gran. It would take forever, and the ambulance would be gone. The men were already passing him, reaching the hall. The oxygen mask covered most of Grandad's face, with bits of mustache sticking out round the rim. His eyes were still open.

"Just tell her Grandad's had a heart attack or something," Gavin said. "They're taking him to the Kincardine. I've got to go. Thanks."

He put the phone down and rushed out into the road. The men were just finishing loading Grandad into the ambulance. Despite the rain, half a dozen people were out on the pavement, watching.

"Can I come too?" he said. "I was with him when it happened. I can tell the doctors. Or I'll walk."

"May as well come," said Mr. Toller. "We're not supposed to leave you alone in the house, anyway."

So Gavin sat beside the driver while the ambulance sped whooping off through the rain. They swung in at the hospital in less than a minute. He followed the stretcher in, but at the reception desk the clerk asked him to stop and tell her stuff like Grandad's name and address and date of birth and so on. He knew the birthday, the second of March, and he worked out the year by subtracting seventy-four from two thousand and three. When he'd finished he asked the clerk to ring Mum's mobile again and tell her what was happening, and she told him where to go next.

He went through two lots of swing doors and found Grandad, still on the stretcher, lying on a sort of table in a small room with a woman in a white coat bending over him and looking into one of his eyes through a sort of torch thing. A nurse who was there collared Gavin and took him into an office and started to ask him a lot more questions about what had happened, making notes as she went on.

Then Gran showed up. Gavin heard her before he saw her, saying something over her shoulder to the clerk at the reception desk as she came through the swing doors. He could tell from the tone of Gran's voice that they knew each other— Gran seemed to know half the people in Stonehaven. They let her go in and see Grandad for a bit, and then they brought her into the office to help with the questions. She was very upset—crying some of the time—but that didn't stop her talking. Grandad was almost never ill, but Gran seemed to remember every little sniffle he'd ever had and wanted to tell the nurse about all of them.

That slowed things up, and before the nurse had finished her questions Mum arrived. She was probably upset too, though Grandad wasn't her father, but it was much harder to tell with Mum. Mum was quite different from Gran. Gran was round and smiley and a bit untidy, in a comfortable kind of way. She was really interested in people and everything about them. Strangers who came into the shop for a pack of hacksaw blades would finish up telling her stuff they mightn't have told their best friend.

Mum always looked smart. She needed to, for her job, but she still did even on holiday. She was slim but not quite skinny and didn't really look like anyone's mum. (Gran looked like everyone's mum.) She liked sorting things out, keeping life tidy and clean and under control. She wasn't exactly bossy, telling Gavin what to do all the time. Provided he had his own life sorted—which he did, mostly, because he didn't like mess either—she left him to it. And if he had the right sort of problem—practical, with things to be done about it—she could be terrific.

Mum didn't normally talk anything like as much as Gran, but a crisis like this made her sort of fizz, like a bottle of fizzy water when you open it carelessly. Plans and ideas were trying to squirt out of her. Now Gavin could see how frustrating it was for her, having to sit and wait while Gran answered the questions, when what Mum wanted to know was what was going to happen next and whether that was the best thing for Grandad and what she was going to do about it if she decided it wasn't.

But it wasn't long before the woman who'd been looking at Grandad came in. She turned out to be Dr. Boone. She wasn't exactly a friend, but Mum had sold her her house and she'd bought stuff from Gran at Hankin's, so they both knew her. This was just as well. Mum had a thing about doctors. Usually she didn't trust them at all. She took a magazine called *What Doctors Don't Tell You*. It was all about doctors getting it wrong and she believed every word of it.

"I'm afraid it looks as if your husband has had a severe stroke, affecting his left side, Mrs. Robinson," said Dr. Boone. "It's a waste of precious time my investigating further. We've only been waiting to hear whether we should send him to the stroke unit at Aberdeen or Perth. They've both been extremely busy. But now a call's come through to say we can send him up to the Royal Victoria, and they'll have a bed for him there by this evening. Even if there's a crisis before that, they'll be able to take better care of him than we could here. He'll be on his way in a couple of minutes. One of you can go with him in the ambulance, if you want, but you'll have to make your own arrangements about getting back."

They all got to their feet. Both Gran and Mum started talking at the same time, Gran thanking Dr. Boone and from force of habit asking her how her collie was, and Mum making arrangements for driving over with Gavin to Aberdeen to bring Gran back and picking up a take-away on the way because it would be better than what they'd get in the hospital and where were they going to meet. They happened to draw breath at the same moment.

"Is he going to die?" said Gavin.

Dr. Boone shook her head.

"I hope not," she said. "This is his first stroke, as far as we know, and he's a very healthy old man. He has a very good chance of making an almost full recovery on his right side, so that he can talk again and do a lot of things for himself. He may well get back most of the use of his left side too. I know he looks awful, Gavin, but he's still your grandfather. He's there, inside."

"Does he know we're here?"

Dr. Boone shook her head, but smiled. "Not really," she said. "Not yet. People who've come through strokes say that at first it's like having a really muddled dream, the sort you have when you're ill. You don't know where you are or what's happening, and everything feels wrong and no one's telling you anything and you've got to get somewhere but you can't remember where, and so on. But in a couple of days or so it'll start coming back to him. Now you'd better hurry, Mrs. Robinson. The ambulance isn't going to wait for you."

Outside the office an orderly was already wheeling Grandad away. The three of them followed the stretcher out of the hospital and watched it being loaded into the ambulance. Grandad was still wearing the oxygen mask. Gran climbed in beside the driver, the doors were shut, and the ambulance went whooping into Arduthie Road.

Mum talked all the way to Aberdeen—everything she could remember about strokes, and what they were going to do now Grandad wouldn't be there for Gavin to come home to after school, and getting over to visit Grandad at the Royal Vic.

Stuff like that. It all made sense, but he barely listened. He was thinking about Grandad, locked inside his body. And having terrible dreams, not knowing where he was or what was going on. That wasn't Grandad. He always knew that sort of stuff. Always.

# 3

They had a dreadful time at the Royal Vic. It was the middle of the afternoon when they got there, and still raining, bucketing down, and the main car park was full because it was a Saturday and everybody was visiting at the same time, so they had to find somewhere else. The Vic was a huge warren of different buildings, and it was a long way back to the main reception. Mum had a big brolly for sheltering clients under, but they'd hardly started when a passing truck slurped through a puddle at speed and drenched them. It was so sudden that Gavin dropped the pizza and the box burst and spilled it out into the gutter. He scooped it up and carried it till they found a litter bin. By that time he had cheesy tomato all over his hands. He'd thought he was too worried to eat, but now that they'd lost the pizza he was starving.

They stopped at the main hospital entrance and cleaned themselves up in the toilets, best they could. Mum came out looking almost as smart and together as usual, but Gavin still looked, and felt, a mess. He was only in his indoor clothes and his shoes and socks were wet through and he was chilled to the bone.

He waited, shivering, while Mum cleaned him up a bit more with tissues and then they had to go out into the rain again and round to the casualty unit, where both clerks at the reception desk were busy with someone else and they had to wait and wait. When it was their turn, the clerk had to telephone to ask about Grandad, and whoever it was at the other end said they'd find out and call back, so all Gavin and Mum could do was wait and wait again.

It must have been at least ten minutes before the message came through. Grandad was still in the casualty unit waiting to be assessed and Saturdays were always busy and it would be a while yet before that happened, because there was a staff shortage. And—the clerk didn't say this, but she obviously meant it—no one had any time for anything that wasn't vital, like letting worried relatives know what was going on. So even Mum could see that the only thing they could do for the moment was go and sit in the waiting room with several other people who were probably in just the same boat as they were. Gran wasn't one of them.

And Mum was still fizzing with plans. Most of what she said was probably sensible, sort of—things like what would happen if they decided there wasn't room for Grandad at the Royal Vic after all and they had to send him on to Inverness, or back down to Perth, or Edinburgh even, because there'd been this case about an old man being shunted around half the hospitals in England, but that had been in the flu crisis last winter . . . and why didn't Gavin go down to the shop in the main lobby and find himself some biscuits or something . . . ?

"I'm not hungry."

"You must be. You haven't had anything since breakfast."

"Well, I'm not."

He was, though. He was starving. But somehow he felt it wasn't right to be eating biscuits while Grandad was lying somewhere terribly ill. He should have been too upset. He was desperately upset already but it wasn't enough.

"Let me see what I've got," said Mum, reaching for her bag. She carried all sorts of emergency stuff in her bag, aspirin, sticking plasters, throat lozenges, folding cutlery, screwdriver, tape measure—you name it, she'd have it.

"No!" Gavin almost shouted, jumping up and striding away as he fought his tears—tears of hunger, of grief, of anger with himself and Mum and everything. They were in a sort of lobby, with a ward on one side and an office on the other. Opposite them was a corridor, but it turned a corner almost at once so Gavin had no idea what lay beyond. But it was the only place to go, so he walked on and peeped round the corner.

It was just more bright-lit corridor with doors opening off it. Halfway along he saw Gran, sitting on a tall stool beside a trolley. He guessed Grandad must be on the trolley, but he couldn't see him from where he was.

Gran looked awful, gray and exhausted and really old, but she saw Gavin and beckoned. He hurried forward, tiptoeing because he was sure he wasn't supposed to be there.

"Stay with him for a bit, will you?" said Gran. "I've got to go to the toilet."

"Is he going to be all right? What's happening?"

"Nothing. They've got him on a monitor, so they'll know if he gets worse. They keep saying they'll be getting him into a bed soon, but they don't. I've been holding his hand. It's all I can do for him. I can't even tell if he knows I'm there."

"I bet you he does," said Gavin. "Mum's out there. She knows where the nearest toilets are."

(Of course she did. She'd asked the clerk on their way in.)

He took Grandad's right hand as soon as Gran let go, and settled himself onto the stool. The hand twitched and fidgeted, the way it had been doing at Stonehaven. Gavin gave it a squeeze, but it didn't seem to notice.

"Hi, Grandad," he said. "How's things?"

There was no answer, of course. Grandad just lay there. He was still wearing an oxygen mask. Clipped to the end of the stretcher was a gray electronic-looking box with a small screen. Three wires ran from it to Grandad's chest. Monitor, it was called, he remembered, just like on a PC, and the pulsing line on the screen was Grandad's heartbeat. There was a drip stand beside the stretcher with a tube going into his left arm. His eyes were still open. Gavin started to worry about that because Grandad couldn't see properly without his specs. Anything that wasn't right in front of his nose would be all blur and mess. He'd think it was all part of the muddled dream Dr. Boone had talked about.

Wait! The specs were in Gavin's shirt pocket, where he'd put them when he'd picked them up off the floor in Grandad's room, just after the stroke had happened. With a stupid, hopeful feeling that something had at last gone right he took them out and fitted them on. As he did so, Grandad blinked.

Gavin's heart leapt. He swung round, looking for someone to tell. A nurse came hurrying out of a door further along the corridor.

20

"He just blinked!" he told her.

"Can't help it," she told him, not slowing down. She vanished round the corner.

Then he just sat there. The hospital was decently warm but he still felt shivery and cold right through. At least the nurse hadn't told him he wasn't allowed there. He relaxed a bit, enough to start feeling hungry again.

Stuff came back to him, things Mum had said in the car when he thought he hadn't been listening. About people with strokes, how you've got to keep stimulating them, showing them things, talking to them. . . .

"It's still raining," he said. "We got really wet, getting here from the car."

He told Grandad about the truck and the pizza disaster, making it as funny as he could. It wasn't fair—none of it had been Mum's fault, but Grandad always secretly enjoyed it when one of her plans came unstuck. Before he'd finished, two nurses came out of another door. They looked surprised when they saw him.

"Hello," said one of them. "Who are you?"

"I'm Gavin. I'm his grandson. Gran asked me to stay with him while she went to the toilets. She's probably talking to Mum in the waiting place now."

"Well, we're ready for him at last."

One of them took hold of the trolley.

"Can I come too?" said Gavin.

"Best not. Why don't you go find your gran and tell her your granddad's gone for assessment and if she asks at the desk they'll tell her where to come."

"All right. Those are his specs. I had them in my pocket. He can't see much without them."

"We'll look after them. See you."

Gavin got off the stool and started back down the corridor. Something very funny was happening. The corridor was moving around, swaying. It must be an earthquake, he thought. Why weren't there any noises? He couldn't keep his balance. He was falling, falling . . .

Dark. He tried to open his eyes. Too bright. He couldn't remember where he was, or why.

"Looks like he's coming round," said a woman's voice. "Just fainted, probably. When did he last eat?"

"Not since breakfast, I think."

That was Mum, and she flooded on. "He was with my father-in-law when it happened, and that was before lunch—they're very close, you see, and of course he was terribly upset and he kept saying he wasn't hungry—I'd bought something to eat on the way here, but . . ."

And then all about the pizza and the truck and getting soaked and so on.

Of course. Gavin remembered what had happened and opened his eyes. He was lying on the floor where he had fallen. Mum was kneeling beside him, and a nurse was crouching on the other side.

"Is Grandad all right?" he whispered. "What happened? I don't remember."

"Your grandfather's fine," said the nurse, "and so are you. You just fainted. Nothing to be ashamed of. Shock and cold and food shortage—enough to knock anyone out. Now we're going to wrap you up warm and fill you with hot sweet tea and sticky cakes—got to get some sugar into your blood, right? As soon as anyone knows anything we'll come and tell you about your granddad. Up you get, then. Take it easy. . . ."

"I'm all right," Gavin muttered as he stood swaying in the corridor, though he would have fallen without the nurse's arm round his shoulders. In spite of what she'd said, he felt deeply ashamed of himself. It seemed dead feeble, passing out like that and wasting everyone's time when they should have been looking after Grandad.

At least Mum didn't say "Told you so." By the time they got back to the waiting area, she was too busy telling him about insulin deficiency.

"Wake up, darling," said Mum's voice. "Here's the doctor at last."

Oh, yes—Grandad, the hospital, fainting, sweet tea and chocolate digestive biscuits—he could still taste them in his mouth. . . .

Mum was standing, so Gavin pulled the blanket off and got up too. Gran and a doctor were just coming into the waiting area. Gran looked utterly exhausted.

"I'm sorry to have kept you so long," said the doctor. He was exhausted too. Gavin could hear the tiredness in his voice. "It's been the hell of a day—always happens at weekends. And I'm afraid there isn't a lot I can tell you yet. We can't be dead certain till we've done the scans, but all the signs tell me your husband's had a fairly severe stroke, Mrs. Robinson, so we're sending him up to the stroke unit. It may not be as bad as it looks at the moment—I've seen patients make almost complete recoveries from where he is now, but it's a slow process. In the next few weeks I'd expect him to regain some control over the right side of his body, and perhaps some power of speech too, but that's a gradual process. He'll be able to understand what you say to him some time before he can answer at all clearly. The left side is more problematic, and it's impossible to say at this stage how much movement he will recover there. It could be anything from very little to almost complete control. The physios will be able to tell you more when they've been working with him for a bit."

"We can help with that too, can't we?" said Mum.

"Sure you can. That's often half the battle. The physios will talk to you about it."

"When can we have him back at the Kincardine?" said Mum. "It'll be much easier for us to visit him there."

"They usually keep patients in the stroke unit for about a month. That allows them to see some recovery and assess how much further they're likely to progress and what level of future care they're going to . . . Yes?"

He had turned away because a nurse had appeared. She muttered briefly to him. Gavin saw his shoulders sag still further before he turned back to them.

"I'm sorry," he said. "I've got to go. I don't think there's any point in your waiting any longer. There's nothing more you can do, and there isn't going to be anything more I can tell you now."

"They'll call us if anything happens?" said Mum.

"Yes, of course. You gave all your details to the reception desk, including your telephone number? Great. Then it'll be going up with him to the stroke unit."

And he hurried away.

Gavin slept most of the way home and had to grope his way in through the door, and then got tangled up with Dodgem, who was capering round Gran, whingeing for his supper. He forced himself to stay awake and eat a bit of cold pie out of the fridge, and then dragged himself up past his bedroom into the attic. As he climbed the last flight he could hear Mum on the phone, trying to reach Dad on the ship satellite system. Last time Dad had called, his ship had just left Trinidad, heading for Panama. As he reached the top of the stairs Gavin heard her get through. Dad would be having his afternoon nap about now, maybe.

He cleaned up the mess of painty turpentine on Grandad's workbench, put the brushes to soak in fresh turps, and made everything as neat as he could. As he groped his way down to bed he could hear Mum trying to find someone in Edinburgh who knew what Donald was doing that weekend.

His last thought as he fell asleep was, I'll finish *Selkie* in time for my birthday.

# 4

Next day was Sunday. Gavin slept late, and when he came down Gran was already on the telephone, telling her friends what had happened. Mum started making plans the moment he came into the kitchen. He half listened as he got his breakfast together.

"It's my Sunday on, darling, and I can't ask Mary or Bob to stand in because they've both got stuff fixed . . ."

(Mum and two other people in her office took turns working on Sundays, showing people houses.)

". . . so Gran's going to take you in to Aberdeen on the train after lunch and I should be off by four so I'll come and pick you up and find out what's going on, if anything. And for tomorrow I'll ask Janet if she can have you after school until Gran gets home, or Bessie McCracken, or—"

"But—" said Gavin. He'd already decided what he wanted to do.

"All right, darling, if you don't get on with Ian I can always ask—"

"No. Please. I get on fine with Ian, but I want to go and see Grandad after school."

"No, darling. I'm sorry, but—"

"Please, Mum. I'll be all right. I wouldn't talk to anybody I didn't know. And Gran can show me today about getting to the Royal Vic. Please. It would be good for Grandad, wouldn't it, having someone with him he knows? Gran can't get there till the evening. And then I can come home with her or you can come and pick us up. Please."

You could make Mum listen if you really tried. She started to shake her head.

"Please," he said again.

"I've got to go. I'll think about it, darling. Tell Gran, in case you want me today, I'll keep my mobile switched on and . . ."

Her good-bye kiss was a sort of punctuation mark in the flow. She was still talking as she went out the front door.

Gran could perfectly well have driven them in to the Royal Vic in Grandad's car, but she hated driving in Aberdeen. Almost as soon as the train pulled out of the station she started telling him about people who'd lived in some of the houses they passed, and their mothers and fathers, and (if the train hadn't come to another house for her to tell him about) grannies and granddads and who'd married who and then run away with who else, and so on. He realized it was only her way of stopping herself thinking about what had happened to Grandad, and Gran's talk could be pretty interesting if you were in the mood, but not now. He wanted to think. He got his homework out and pretended to be doing it, but that didn't make any difference. In the end he put his homework away and waited for a chance to interrupt her.

"Gran?"

"Yes, darling. What is it?"

"Do you know anyone who goes from Stonehaven to

27

Aberdeen every afternoon? After school, so I can go and visit Grandad without having to wait for you? I'm sure I could go on my own, but Mum's not going to let me."

"I don't know what we're coming to. Your age, I was on the bus out to Muchalls on my own for my piano lessons in the evening, Tuesdays, regular as clockwork, and that meant home in the dark wintertime, with the lighting nothing like so good as they've got it now, not that I couldn't've gone to Carrie Lennox—she was in Slug Road then, just a wee step away, but my mam had had words with her over us missing choir practice—those days we were all Auld Kirk, of course—so it was the bus to Muchalls for me, and Mr. McPhee, with his sister sitting in the corner so that none of us girls could make trouble saying he'd been stroking our knees or something, poor wee man, and to think he'd played in a concert once in front of the queen . . ."

"Gran?"

"Yes, darling."

"Somebody to take me to Aberdeen after school."

"I'm thinking, darling. Colin Smith could've done it, but he's been dead this eighteen years, since the train hit his van on the level crossing, hurrying, it came out, because of not wanting his boss to know he was taking a detour to visit Fiona Murray up at her dad's farm . . ."

And so on, all the way to Aberdeen. There was a bus direct from the station to the Royal Vic. Gavin could see it would be as easy as pie if only Mum would let him.

The stroke unit was upstairs, in a different building from the one with the casualty unit in it. It had a lobby with a reception

28

desk and a short corridor with several wards opening off it. Grandad's bed was in the corner of one of the wards. There were five other beds, all with somebody in them. A woman in a white coat—a doctor, Gavin guessed—was watching the dials on a bit of equipment beside one of the beds and making notes; and a nurse was standing at the head of one of the other beds slowly massaging the head and neck of the person in it. This was a woman who didn't look any older than Mum. She was rather pretty, in fact, except that her skin was kind of grayish.

There were curtains to go round Grandad's bed, but they were drawn back. Grandad was lying half on his side, propped in place with a pillow behind him. There was a short tube going into one nostril with a stopper at its other end, and wires from his chest to the monitor at the foot of his bed, and a drip feed. His right hand kept plucking at a button on his pajamas until Gran grabbed hold of it and held it. They'd only given him one pillow, so that even if he'd had his specs on he wouldn't have been able to see much. Ceilings aren't that interesting. All the same, Gavin looked in the locker beside the bed, found the specs, and put them on him. Grandad blinked again, but his eyes still didn't move. There was something funny about the blink, but Gavin couldn't see what.

Gran was already telling Grandad about all the people she'd called, and what they'd said. Gavin wondered if Grandad was listening. There aren't a lot of different ways of saying how sorry you are, and Grandad was used to tuning Gran out, just grunting now and then to show she wasn't talking to a brick wall. Not that he could even do that now. Gavin got out his homework and started in on it for real.

After a bit Gran went off to see if she could find a nurse who'd tell her what was happening, so Gavin took hold of the fidgety hand and with his other hand got out the *Model Boats* he'd brought and read Grandad bits of that. It was last month's, so Grandad must have read it already, but he often read things two or three times if they interested him. There was a long article about a big show at Dortmund, in Germany, with hundreds of boats in it. Some of them were the sort Grandad used to build, not out of kits he'd bought in a box but making all the pieces himself. Scratch-built, it was called. There was one man who'd spent five years on a strange sort of fishing boat and hadn't finished yet. That sounded amazing.

Gavin didn't read the article straight off in one go, just a sentence or two, and then a pause, and then another short bit, as if it were something he was reading to himself, and telling Grandad the interesting bits. That made it sound a bit more like what used to happen when they were alone together. He'd have needed to keep pausing anyway, because of the way his eyes couldn't help misting up.

Gran came back eventually. She'd been so long because the ward sister had an aunt in Stonehaven, somebody Gran knew, and they'd talked about her a wee bit (one of Gran's wee bits) as well as what was happening with Grandad. There wasn't anything new, this still being the weekend. He was booked for a scan the next day, and then the doctors would be able to see how much damage there was inside his brain. At the moment all they could say was that it looked as if it was in the part that controlled his left side, and his right side might be okay in the end.

Being Gran, she spun it all out, with plenty of side turnings and goings-back—all about the sister's aunt in Stonehaven, and so on. She'd taken over from Gavin, holding the fidgety hand, so he'd gone round to the far side of the bed to hold Grandad's left hand—the one that might never be any good again. This hand felt different, not exactly floppy, not dead, but not alive either. Like a turned-off TV—there's always a faint hum when the set's on, too quiet to notice, but when the set's off you can tell the difference. Like that.

Gavin didn't just hold the hand. He played with it as he sat and half listened to Gran, moving the fingers about, helping it to fidget like the other one, giving it something to think about, he hoped. And perhaps a few tiny crumbs of that something might find their way through to Grandad where he lay locked in his frozen body—a bit like a story Mr. Garton had given Gavin to read last term, about a man who'd been thrown into prison somewhere long ago, all by himself in a tiny dark cell, until he'd heard a faint tapping sound coming along a pipe on the wall. And the man had tapped back in answer to let whoever it was at the other end of the pipe know he was there.

Of course, no answer came back through Grandad's hand. That would have been too much to hope for. Yet.

Mum didn't show up till almost eight o'clock. And of course she needed to see the sister too, and find out exactly what was going on, and make sure it was the right thing—she'd been checking out strokes on the Web the night before until after midnight—so by the time they were back in Stonehaven it was much too late for Gavin to go out to the harbor alone.

There was something he felt he had to do as soon as possible. It had come to him while he was sitting by Grandad's bed, remembering over and over again the awful moment of Grandad's stroke, happening so suddenly, out of nowhere. One moment Grandad had been putting his brushes away, relaxing, talking playfully about selkies, and the next . . .

It was like something he'd seen once on TV, a terrorist bomb going off in a peaceful street, and everything changing. The telly only showed the mayhem afterward, the mess, the ambulances. The people running around screaming. But something must have happened just before, triggering the explosion. What?

Grandad had asked Gavin if he'd thought of a name for the trawler, Gavin had suggested *Selkie,* and Grandad had agreed, and then . . .

*"No harm in having the selkies on your side—they'll give you a hand if you're in trouble. But they can be touchy too, if the stories have them right. You'd best go down to the bay and ask them if they mind."*

When he went to bed Gavin set his alarm an hour early and put it under his pillow so that it didn't wake Mum or Gran up to come out and tell him no.

It was a still, pearly dawn, with the sea barely rippling against the harbor wall. There was no one about, apart from one or two joggers on their way to the main seafront, where most of them ran. Gavin didn't really believe in what he was going to do. It was just something he could do—the *only* thing he could do—for Grandad. That seemed to make it better than not doing it. Near as he could find it, he chose the exact spot he'd been standing when the seal had popped its head out of the water.

"Selkie," he whispered. "I'm sorry. I'm really sorry. I should have asked you first. But please may I name my boat after you? She's really beautiful. She belongs in the water. It's her home. She's like you.

"And if you can do something for Grandad . . ."

His voice trailed away, leaving him feeling ashamed of himself for trying anything so stupid.

He trudged back up to Arduthie Road and let himself quietly in. Gran was in the kitchen in her dressing gown, drinking her early tea and reading her horoscope aloud to Dodgem, and Mum was having her shower. Gavin got Mum's orange juice out of the fridge and set it to unchill for her, and then made himself breakfast, just as he would have done any other day.

# 5

School started badly. Gavin was pretty depressed even before he got there at the thought of having to wait for Gran to take him to Aberdeen, and so being with Grandad for hardly any time at all before they had to go home, and Gran talking the whole way through. And then, just after assembly, the headmaster, Mr. Henryson, sent for him to say Mum had called to explain about Grandad, and how sorry he was. And when Gavin got back to his class he could tell at once from the way the other kids looked at him, or didn't, that Mrs. Brenner had been telling them too while he was out of the room, and probably saying to go easy on him, or whatever.

It had to be like that, Gavin guessed, and anyway the kids probably knew already. Mr. Toller, the ambulance man, would have told Garry—bound to—and trust Garry to spread it around. But yuck! What had happened to Grandad was private, private, private, but now he'd got to creep into class with everyone knowing, feeling sorry for him maybe—fat lot of good that did, now!—or just inquisitive, or embarrassed, which was what he'd have felt, he guessed, if it had happened to one of the others. . . .

After that it got better. The classwork was something else to think about—most of the time, anyway—and once or twice when he started brooding Mrs. Brenner must have noticed, and she managed to break it up for him without obviously picking him out.

Out of class the kids reacted in different ways. The ones he didn't know that well were mostly plain shy of talking to him, or even looking at him, which was fine by Gavin. His own friends said they were really sorry—they all liked Grandad—and Gavin said thanks, but he didn't want to talk about it; and then he wished he hadn't, because he'd have liked to talk to someone and there wasn't anyone at home. He didn't want to hang around with them either, with them trying to be nice to him and him feeling he was spoiling things for them, so he sneaked off to the library and read bits of a Harry Potter he'd read twice already.

When Gavin came out of school he found his brother, Donald, waiting for him. Mum had been trying to call Don but he hadn't answered, so Gavin hadn't been expecting him. He was supposed to go back with Ian to Mrs. McCracken's and wait for Gran to come and take him to Aberdeen so he didn't even notice Donald standing among the usual gang of parents outside the school.

"Hi, Gav. Don't want to know me these days?"

"Don! But . . ."

"Why don't you find your friend and tell him you're coming with me, and then we'll hop in Grandad's car and go and see how the old boy's getting on. You can tell me all about it in the car. We can't talk on my bike. Okay?"

So only a few minutes later they were whizzing up the A92 at twice the speed Grandad ever drove. Gavin had never been quite sure where he was with his brother. Donald was twelve years older than him, and had somehow never really felt like part of the family. It was funny. Dad was away so much that when Gavin was small he had sometimes forgotten what he looked like by the time he came home again, but still Dad slotted in and belonged, in a way that Donald didn't seem to, though he'd lived at home then.

People always told Gavin that he could tell what he was going to look like when he was grown up—they meant fair-haired, blue-eyed, not very tall, maybe a bit pudgy, but sturdy with it—because he took after Dad so much, and Dad took after Grandad, though he didn't have a mustache. But Donald took after Mum, tall, lean, dark, impatient. Maybe that was why he and Mum used to fight so much. Maybe too it was why he'd decided to become a doctor. Mum had been absolutely furious about that, and it was still a sore point, so Donald didn't come home much, except when Dad was going to be there too.

As soon as they were clear of Stonehaven Donald dropped his jaunty manner.

"This is a bad deal," he said. "Poor old boy. I'm really fond of Grandad, you know. You were with him when it happened, Mum said. Care to tell me?"

So Gavin told him the whole story in its proper order, leaving nothing out except his visit to the harbor that morning. He even put in the bit about himself fainting in the hospital, though he was still deeply ashamed of that. Donald didn't interrupt at all.

"Lucky you were there," he said when Gavin had finished. "Sounds like you got it about right. He was down for a scan today, you said. That'll tell us a bit more."

36

"When will they know if he's going to get better?"

"They won't, not until it happens. He should start controlling his right-side movement in two or three days, the leg before the arm usually. . . ."

"He keeps fidgeting with his hand. All the time. He doesn't seem to know he's doing it. It's horrible."

"Happens, Gav. A lot of this is going to be pretty upsetting for anyone who knew him before. Same when he starts trying to talk—he won't have any control of that either. Just grunts and gasps. And don't forget he'll find it incredibly tiring. For a long while everything's going to be a huge effort for him—stuff you and I do without thinking. The lines are down all over Grandad's body, Gav. You want to scratch your nose, your brain gets on the phone to your arm and tells it, 'Scratch nose,' and *pow!*, your arm's moving. Grandad's brain knows what it wants, just as much as yours, but all it can do is scribble a message on a bit of scrap paper and give it to whoever chances by. And even then the poor guy has got to find his way across country. Not nice tame country, either. Country after an earthquake—floods in the valleys, avalanches blocking the passes. Brain's going to lose a lot of messengers, and when one finally does get through he's going to find the proper nose-scratching machinery's been smashed in the earthquake and he'll have to jury-rig something out of bits and pieces and do the best he can with that.

"We can all do a bit to help, but it's going to be mainly down to Grandad himself what kind of recovery he makes—him and the physios."

"What are physios?"

"Physiotherapists. Straight physiologists tell you what exercises to do when you've injured your leg or something, and you want to get it working again. Physiotherapists do that with the brain. They'll look at the scans and the external signs of brain damage, and then try to teach the undamaged parts to take over some of the functions of the damaged parts. A really good physio can make all the difference."

There was only one nurse in the ward this time, sitting on a chair and writing on a pad on her knee. She glanced up when they came in and went back to her writing. Someone had clipped Grandad's mustache—it looked very strange—but apart from that Gavin couldn't see any change in him. He was still lying there, on his back, with the tube going into his nose and the wires fastened to his chest. Donald studied the monitor for a bit, and read the notes on the clipboard beside it.

They'd taken Grandad's specs away, of course. Gavin found them and put them on him, and while he was doing it Grandad blinked. This time Gavin was ready and saw what was funny about the blink.

"His eye didn't shut properly when he blinked."

"That's right," said Donald, not looking up.

"But it was his right eye, and it's his left side that's gone wonky."

"It's the right side of his brain that's shot. Controls that side of his face, but then it crosses over and does the other side of his body. . . . Nothing about the scan here. Details won't have come up yet, supposing they've done it. I'll go and see. You'll be okay?"

38

"Yes, of course. Can I draw the curtains? It'll feel more like I'm alone with him, the way we usually are."

"Better not," said Donald as he lounged off. "Nurse needs to be able to check on him."

He sounded surprised, amused, sympathetic, all at the same time.

Gavin felt frustrated. He'd been planning to perch himself on the bed, where Grandad could see him, and he was fairly sure he wasn't supposed to, which was the real reason he'd wanted the curtains drawn. Best he could do was get hold of Grandad's fidgeting hand and stand and lean over the bed, which wasn't very comfortable. He'd packed another *Model Boats* in his satchel, but he didn't get it out at once. Instead he told Grandad about going down to the harbor that morning to ask the selkie for permission to name the trawler after it.

"I felt really stupid about it," he said. "I still do. I'm not going to tell anyone else about it, but . . ."

As his voice trailed away the hand stopped trying to fidget and something seemed to change in the still, blue eyes—a flicker, a gleam, barely there for an instant, then gone.

His heart missed a beat. He waited, holding his breath, but the gleam didn't come back. Grandad's hand let go of his own. . . .

Grandad's hand let go of his own . . . ?

Grandad had been holding his hand!

It hadn't been just a fidget that felt like that—it had really happened.

When?

Just when the gleam came, it must have been—he'd have

noticed at once, earlier. So it was only for a moment. Like the gleam, there and gone. Both almost nothing, but for Gavin they changed everything. Grandad had heard him, and understood. *He* didn't think talking to the selkie was stupid, if it was what Gavin wanted to do. Until now, whatever people had said to him, he had never really believed in his heart that he would get Grandad back. Now, in that glimmer, that soft grasp, he had seen that he could.

He looked up for someone to tell the news to, but the nurse was on the telephone now. He could tell from the way she was doing it, laughing a bit, moving her free hand around, shrugging her shoulders, that she was chatting to a friend, so she might be going on for ages. He turned back to Grandad.

"Hi, Grandad, that was great. You heard me, didn't you, talking about going to the harbor and saying thank you to the selkie . . . ?"

Nothing. The blue eyes stayed blank. No, not nothing. The hand . . .

The hand wasn't trying to fidget anymore. It didn't even twitch. But it still felt all right, like Grandad's hand, not like the other one, only as if he'd napped off for a bit. When Gavin let go the fingers opened slightly, as if they were making themselves comfortable in their new position, and lay still.

He looked at the nurse, but she was still chatting away, so he took hold of Grandad's hand again and started to tell him instead, saying how exciting it was, just knowing Grandad was there, inside his body, and had heard him. But this time there wasn't any response at all, nothing he could feel or see, and his voice began to trail away, so after a bit he used his foot to pull the chair as close as he could get and sat down and read bits of Model Boats in a low voice so as not to disturb the other patients. For some reason that little burst of excitement seemed to have left him feeling extraordinarily tired and dispirited. It was difficult not to mutter, as if he were only reading aloud to himself. He had to keep thinking of Grandad, really there inside that dead-seeming body, listening to every word.

When he looked up for a rest he saw that the nurse had stopped writing and was watching him. His heart sank as she rose and came over.

"I'm sorry," he said. "Am I making too much noise?"

"No, is fine," she said. "What you read him?"

He blinked. He hadn't realized she was foreign. She looked perfectly ordinary, dark-haired, with a rather bony face. She had a nice smile. He showed her Model Boats.

"He held my hand for a moment," he said. "And now it's stopped trying to move around. Is that all right?"

"Of course. He is asleep now."

Gavin had been sitting too low to see Grandad's face properly. Startled, he half rose and saw that, yes, the lids were closed over the blue eyes. He felt a bit of a fool, reading all this time to a sleeping man, but maybe Grandad understood him just as well in his dreams as he did waking. And it was a huge relief to see him peaceful at last.

The nurse was still looking at Model Boats.

"Is funny for kid to read," she said.

"It's what Grandad reads at home," he explained. "He makes the most beautiful boats. He was making one for my birthday when he had his stroke. He'd almost finished. It was going to be lovely."

"I like to see it."

"Okay, I'll bring some photos in when I've finished her," he said. "It might do a bit of good, him just seeing them. Remind him. Who he is, I mean. He's there—I'm sure he's there, only he doesn't know what's going on. That's why I'm reading *Model Boats* to him. To remind him. I can't do that while the others are here, and they won't let me come alone. We spend a lot of time together when we're at home. I'm . . . I'm what he's used to. . . . I'm right to try, aren't I?"

He stopped because his voice had gone croaky. The nurse was still smiling.

"Best you talk to physio," she said, and went back to her writing.

Fat chance, Gavin thought, with Mum or Gran there. He started reading *Model Boats* again, but almost at once Gran showed up, telling Donald over her shoulder all about Cathy Munro at work, and how she'd come in on her afternoon off just so Gran could get away and catch an early train to Aberdeen, which meant she and Gavin could go back by train and Mum didn't need to drive over. Gavin gave her his chair and moved down to the foot of the bed and started in on his homework. After a bit Donald got tired of listening to Gran and said he'd got to get back to Edinburgh and he'd like to see Mum on the way. Gavin said he'd go with him. He felt a bit guilty about this—he'd had Grandad all to himself for half an afternoon, hadn't he? It was Gran's turn now, surely. But he couldn't help minding.

"Did they tell you anything?" Gavin said as they were walking out across the car park.

"Bit. I had a word with the physio. They're still working on the scans, so they're not saying anything definite yet, but I had a look too. They're not that promising, I'm afraid, Gav. I only know what I've been taught, mind, but even I can see there's a fair amount of damage. The actual damage would have happened pretty suddenly, but sometimes there are warning signs. They haven't got his GP's notes yet. Did he say anything about having the odd little blackout?"

"No, but he wouldn't. He might've gone to Dr. Moray, but he'd have kept it to himself. Does it mean he's not going to get better after all?"

"You can't say that. Chances are he'll get better, but maybe not as much as we hoped. Astonishing things happen, mind you, and he's a determined old bird."

"But, suppose it's only a bit better . . . or not at all . . . ?"

"Well . . ."

They had reached the car. Donald paused, jiggling the key ring up and down in his palm.

"Please, Don. I've got to know. Don't try and be kind, like everyone else is doing."

"Okay, kid. Normal form is they'll keep him in the stroke unit for a month, with the physios working on him, and at the end of that time they'll assess where he's got to. If he's made no improvement at all, or very little, they'll move him out to a general ward, probably to the Kincardine if they've got room for him, so you can visit him easier. He'll be looked after there okay—it's a good little hospital—but the chances are he won't last long. If he's still making definite progress after a month they'll keep him on in the stroke unit, if they can spare the bed, and go on working on him. After that, there's a range of options, depending how much care he needs. He could go into a home with full-time care, or he could go home to Arduthie Road with some care coming in, or if he's done really well he could simply go home, though that would mean shuffling the house around so he's got a room on the ground floor, and so on. If you want me to guess, I should think you'd have him home in the end, with Gran working part-time and someone else coming in to cover for her. Right?"

"Thanks, Don."

They got into the car and drove off in silence. Gavin didn't feel as depressed as he might have been. He'd seen that gleam, that flicker of the real Grandad, behind the unanswering eyes. And Grandad had held his hand, known he was there. It was a bit like that moment down at the harbor when the seal had blinked at him as if it understood what he was saying, he thought. And then it had dived out of sight and you'd never have known it was there. But it had still been there, some-where below the surface. And Grandad was still there too.

Perhaps Gavin was the only person who really believed that, he thought. And maybe that meant he was the only person who could get Grandad back. How? How to be alone with him for a while, day after day, when it would always be Gran tak-ing Gavin to Aberdeen and Mum coming to fetch them . . . ?

44

"What's the physio like, Don?"

"Fine. Obviously knows her stuff, but human with it. They're a pretty good bunch on the whole."

"Do you think you could persuade her to tell Mum it's a good idea for me to be alone with Grandad some of the time?"

"You want him for just yourself?"

"Course not. But . . ."

Gavin hesitated. Donald hadn't sounded disapproving, just amused and surprised, but he was right too, in a way. Maybe there *was* something a bit selfish about thinking he was the only one who could really help Grandad, get through to him. Still . . .

"I'm what he's used to, you see," he said. "We don't talk a lot, so he listens to me when I say something. Mum and Gran will just go and sit by his bed and talk and talk and talk, but that's no help because he's used to shutting them out."

Donald laughed.

"I suppose it's a point," he said. "I'll brood on it."

Gavin plowed on. He could hear from Donald's voice that he was being pushy about this, but he'd thought the whole thing through, over and over, and he couldn't have stopped it coming out, even if he'd wanted to.

"Don't try and tell Mum yourself," he said. "You'll just get into a row. But if you could get onto Dad and get him to say to Mum that it's okay for me to go over on the train after school. And then Mum and Gran wouldn't have to rush away from work but one of them could come over and be with Grandad for a bit and bring me back. . . ."

"Okay, okay—you'll be telling the consultant what to do

next. Look, I was going to call Dad anyway—tell him about the scan. I'll see what he says."

"Great. You can e-mail me on Grandad's PC. I've got an address there. I'll write it down."

Gavin watched Donald roar away on his motorbike, then went in and got a take-away lamb stew out of the freezer. Mum always said supermarket instant meals were full of chemicals and stuff, but she'd stocked up with them for now, while they were having to go over to Aberdeen most evenings. Gavin guessed she secretly preferred instants to real cooking anyway.

The sound of the freezer door woke Dodgem from his normal stupor, so to make up, sort of, for wanting to have Grandad all to himself when he mattered just as much to Gran, Gavin took Dodgem out on the usual snail's-pace round to sniff at every other gatepost for doggie messages and leave his own messages on top of them. That left just enough time to go up to the attic and put a final coat on *Selkie*'s wheelhouse.

# 6

After all that it was Gran who really did the trick, but Don helped too. When she picked Gavin up from Mrs. McCracken's next day she started telling him pretty well at once about Katie Wilson who dispensed the medicines at Boots and what a bright kid she'd been—mad about chemistry, and getting a scholarship to Cambridge University and how everyone had expected her to go on and get to be a professor and win the Nobel Prize and so on, but all she'd really wanted to do was come back and live in Stonehaven and marry Bobby Wilson and have six children only she couldn't because Bobby, despite him being such a fine upstanding lad to look at, had a sperm count which was pretty well zilch, but they adopted anyway and seeing them together with the kids you wouldn't ever guess it if you'd not been told.

That lasted them till they got to the station. Gavin tuned most of it out, though other times he might have been interested because Tod Wilson had been in Arduthie Primary till last year, though Gavin hadn't had much to do with him, being a couple of years younger. Gran had to stop to buy the tickets and ask the clerk whether their cat had had kittens yet and had they found the homes for them because she knew some people they might ask, and that lasted till the train came in.

Then it was back to Katie Wilson and her friend Nan who used to work at Boots only now she worked in the dispensary at Aberdeen General Hospital, and Gavin started paying attention, though he still had to sift out stuff about Nan's brother Tom who was a champion bagpiper only he'd married this Dutch lassie who couldn't bear the sound of the pipes, and so on. But by the time they reached Aberdeen he'd got all the stuff that mattered. Katie's friend Nan worked the early shift in the dispensary. The man who did the late shift was called Robert, and he lived at Catterline, just down the coast. The changeover time was five o'clock, so he'd be coming past Stonehaven on the bypass a bit after four o'clock. It wouldn't be more than a few minutes out of his way for him to come by the school and pick Gavin up and take him direct to the hospital.

"Oh, Gran, that's great!" he said. "Thanks so much! That was clever of you."

"Some use, sometimes, knowing one or two people," she said. "And I daresay you'll do Grandad more good than either me or your ma would. He's forgotten how to listen to me, you know. Trouble is, the more I say the more he doesn't listen, and the more he doesn't listen the more I say, and neither of us can help it somehow. Ah, well, I suppose it's better than quarreling all the time the way some folks do. Remember Betty and Bruce Stickling? . . . No, of course you wouldn't. . . ."

The Sticklings lasted her all the way up to the ward and while they were waiting outside because there was stuff going on with one of the other patients. Gavin found he was thinking a bit differently about Gran now. He hadn't got how miserable she was, underneath, but there'd been something in her voice just before she'd started telling him about the Sticklings. . . .

Quietly he took her hand. She stopped what she was going to say and looked down at him, surprised.

"I'm sorry, Gran," he whispered.

"What about, darling?"

"Grandad not listening to you any more."

"No need, darling. We've had a very good life together, and I daresay it's my fault as much as it's his. He's a lovely man, I still think."

"Do you think you could tell Mum what you said—about it being good for him to be alone with me? I think she's still going to take a bit of persuading, you see. She'll say stuff about not knowing Robert, and so on."

Gran smiled, pursing her lips. Gavin could see her starting to plan her campaign.

Mum came and fetched them. She said Dad had called, saying he'd be home the weekend after next, while his ship was in port.

They picked up a pizza on the way home and microwaved it, so supper was almost instant. Gran didn't say anything about Robert, and it wasn't Gavin's turn to wash up, so as soon as he'd cleared his dirties he said he had homework to do. In fact he'd done most of it at Mrs. McCracken's, waiting for Gran, which meant he could go upstairs and start doing the last little bits of touching up on *Selkie*'s stand.

Grandad had made it out of a bit of bookshelf he'd got out

of a skip, so there were a few tiny scratches here and there, and a couple of deeper ones. Gavin used a knife blade to squidge in a little ready-mixed filler from a tube, and while he waited for it to dry enough for sanding he thought about how to do the name. He was worried about getting it neat enough, and the same each time—once each side of the bow and again on the stern with the name of the home port, Stonehaven, below.

The first thing, he thought, was to experiment on the PC to find letters that looked right. While he was at it he looked to see if there was anything from Donald on Grandad's e-mail. There wasn't, but there were several messages from Grandad's model-making cronies about different things. There was no reason they could have known what had happened to Grandad, but it still felt amazing that they didn't. He e-mailed them back, telling them, and asking them to keep writing, and printed their letters out to read to Grandad the next day.

Next morning while Gavin was making his sandwiches for lunch Mum said, "Gran's found somebody to drive you into Aberdeen after school. He actually works in the hospital, and he's going to call in at my office on his way past and I'll come up with him and make sure you meet up. I've got to say I'm still not entirely happy about this—I mean, it's not as if it's some-one we know. . . ."

"I bet you Gran knows more about him than his own mum does. Like Don says, it's a good thing she never went in for blackmail."

Mum laughed but shook her head.

"I'm afraid you can't ever tell," she said. "Men you'd've thought were absolutely safe . . ."

"I'll be really careful, Mum. And I'll tell you if anything at all funny happens. Promise."

"That's what I was going to ask you. All right. Now, they don't want kids wandering all over the hospital unattended, but I've talked to the ward sister, and she's going to leave a message with reception to let you go up. Her name's Sister Taylor, if there's any problems."

(That was typical Mum. Knowing how the system worked, thinking it all out and knowing what to do.)

"Thanks, Mum. That's great. It's what I really wanted."

"Yes, I know, darling," she said, turning away. It was the way she did it, more than anything in her voice, that told him. She didn't want him to see her face, because that would have told him that since she'd talked to Donald she was beginning to worry about him hoping too much. (That was typical Mum too.) Perhaps Donald had told her stuff he hadn't told Gavin, or perhaps she was just worrying because she was like that, worrying about how much he'd mind if Grandad didn't get better, and the more he hoped and hoped the more he'd mind. She was right, of course, but it wasn't going to be like that. It absolutely wasn't.

Robert was a tall, thin man with sunken cheeks and bushy black eyebrows. His big, bony fingers were yellow with tobacco, and his noisy little Datsun reeked of smoke, though he had the windows down, and Mum must have spoken to him about not smoking because he kept one a bit open all the way to Aberdeen. He drove almost as fast as Donald and didn't talk at all. He took Gavin up to the hospital entrance and waited for him to get out.

"Thank you very much," said Gavin as he opened the door. "That's wonderful."

"Glad to help," said Robert. "Same time tomorrow?"

"Yes, please, if that's all right."

Robert nodded, waited for Gavin to get out, and reached a long arm across to close the door. Standing at the entrance to let a wheelchair out, Gavin looked back and saw that he hadn't driven off but was finishing lighting a cigarette.

Mum's arrangements worked. The woman in reception knew about him, and let him sign in and gave him a pass saying he was going up to the stroke unit. When he got to the ward there was a woman he hadn't seen before standing by Grandad's bed. He waited in the doorway, watching, not sure whether to go on in. She was gray haired but not all that old, with a soft, rather anxious-looking face. She was wearing the usual hospital overall, so she wasn't a nurse, but she didn't look quite like a doctor either. She seemed to be doing something with Grandad's right arm—the one that had kept fidgeting about—bending the forearm slowly up, saying a few words, waiting, and then laying the arm back down on the bed. Another few words, and wait, and she started to do it again, but this time she happened to glance up and saw Gavin in the doorway. She smiled again, finished the process, and came over.

"You're Gavin," she said. "I'm Lena. I'm the physio. I was talking to your brother about you this morning. Hi."

"Oh, hello," said Gavin. "Do you want me to go and wait outside till you've finished?"

Lena almost laughed.

"No, of course not," she said. "I want to talk to you. Your brother says he thinks you might help."

"Oh, great! Anything, if you'll show me how. So far I've just been holding his hand and telling him stuff—the sort of things we'd talk about at home."

"That's all useful," she said. "Come and see."

She led the way over to the bed, back to where she'd been before, so Gavin went round to the other side. Nothing seemed to have changed. The blue eyes were open, gazing blankly at the ceiling.

"Hi, Grandad," he said. "I got a lift over. That's why I'm early. This is Lena. She's the physio. She's trying to help you. . . . Is it all right if I put his specs on? He can't see anything without them. I mean, if he's confused already . . . And it makes him look like *him*, except for his mustache being so short."

"Can't hurt now, I suppose," said Lena. "We took them off before, because otherwise he'd have had them off and probably dropped them on the floor and broken them, but now . . . I expect you noticed when you came before that his right arm—this one—wouldn't stop moving about, but he wasn't doing it on purpose. That's called ataxia—it's fairly normal, and as the patient improves it tends to quieten down. But in your grandfather's case it seems to have stopped overnight, and that is a bit unusual. . . ."

"It was quicker than that," said Gavin. "It happened when I was here."

"Tell me."

"Well, I was standing where you are, leaning a bit over the bed so he could see me, and telling him about . . . er, well, stuff that had been happening. I'd got hold of his hand to stop it fidgeting about, though it was still trying to, and I was stroking it on the back with my thumb because that seemed to help, but I wasn't noticing about it because I was thinking about what I was telling him, so I'm not exactly sure when it happened, but all of a sudden I realized it had stopped trying to fidget anymore. And it wasn't just that. He was actually holding my hand."

"Holding it?"

"Yes. I mean . . . Look."

Gavin held his right hand out, palm up, laid his left hand around it, and curled his left fingers gently down beside his right thumb.

"I was holding his hand like this—it was the other way round, actually, but I can't do that on my own hand—anyway, Grandad wasn't doing anything—hadn't been, I mean—but then . . ."

He curled his right fingertips up against the far side of his other hand.

". . . I felt them first, actually, pressing against my hand—not hard, just a bit, and it was only for a moment. Then he let go. They weren't pressing any more."

"You're sure? You don't think it might have been something you made happen. By gripping his hand tighter, for instance?"

Gavin experimented with his own hands.

"No, it doesn't work like that. Look. The fingers sort of

squeeze together, but Grandad's were loose. I'm sure they were."

He waited. Lena didn't say anything for a bit. Then . . .

"That's very interesting. You say it was only for a moment?"

"Well, I'm not sure when it started. You see, I was telling him this stuff and I was actually looking into his eyes, and . . . they *changed*. There was something—a sort of glint—I don't know—perhaps I only imagined it—it was just for a moment, and . . . and . . . well, I kind of knew he was there, listening, him, Grandad . . . I'm sorry. . . ."

To his shame, he was crying, in front of this stranger. Not sobbing or groaning or anything, but tears flooding silently down his cheeks, dripping off his nose and chin . . . He couldn't see anything. . . . Lena was saying something. . . .

". . . didn't imagine it, Gavin. I've seen it too, sometimes, in other patients of mine. I'm not sure it isn't the main reason why I do this job, for that moment, that glimmer of a signal getting through. It makes me feel, however hopeless the case seems, that there's still a chance of getting the real person back in the end. And remember, this is still early days with your granddad. He's had a severe stroke, but it's far too soon to give up on him.

"Now here's some tissues, and you can dry yourself up, and when you're ready we'll try something else together."

She waited while Gavin, full of shame, scrubbed angrily at the drying tears.

"Okay," he muttered. "Sorry about that. I'm all right now."

"Nothing to be sorry about, Gavin. Crying's often the best thing you can do. Now, let me show you. I'm doing two things at the same time. Mainly, at this stage, it's just a matter of exercising his body as much as I can, maintaining the muscle tone, not letting it get into bad habits, but at the same time I'm trying to help him begin to remember how to move about for himself, on purpose. Let me show you. . . .

"Now, Robbie, we're just going to show Gavin how we do your arm exercises. Let's see if you can touch your nose with your right hand. First, I'll do it for you, to remind you, shall I?"

She straightened Grandad's arm beside his body, took hold of his wrist with her right hand, and, holding his elbow in place with her other hand, lifted his forearm gently up and over until the tips of his fingers rested against his nose.

"Good," she said. "Now I'll put it back, and you see if you can do it for yourself. . . . Ready? . . . Now! Come on, Robbie. You can do it. Touch your nose. . . ."

Nothing happened, but Lena didn't seem bothered. She looked up, smiling.

"It's very early days. I wasn't really expecting a response yet. You'll promise not to be disappointed if nothing happens, won't you?"

"All right. You want me to try now?"

"Why not? It isn't difficult. What it really takes is patience, and more patience, and yet more patience, and I really never have time to give everyone all the help I'd like to. That's why people like you can be so useful."

Gavin had moved round to Lena's side of the bed while she was talking, and she'd made room for him. Automatically he'd picked up Grandad's hand and laid it across his body, the way he usually did, so that he could still be holding it comfortably while he was leaning over the bed chatting to him. He hadn't even noticed himself doing it. Now, he looked down, surprised to see the two hands lying there, one across the other. A thought struck him.

"Can I try something else first?" he said.

Lena was amused.

"If you like," she said.

He leaned further over so that he could see into Grandad's eyes.

"Lena's going to show me how to help you with your exercises, Grandad," he said. "But first, before we start, just see if you can take hold of my hand, like you did yesterday when I was telling you what I'd said to the selkie."

It happened. There was no gleam in Grandad's eyes that Gavin could see, but for a moment, and another moment, he felt the faint pressure of fingertips against the side of his own palm. Then it was gone.

He let out a long breath of relief and looked up at Lena.

"Did you see?" he whispered. "It was a bit more than that yesterday."

"Indeed I did," she said. "Though the movement was very slight, and I wouldn't like, at this stage, to swear that he was doing it on purpose. But let's take it for the moment as an encouraging sign. Why don't you see if you can get him to do it again?"

"If you like. All right. . . . That was wonderful, Grandad. Now let's see if you can do it again. I'm going to squeeze your hand, and then you squeeze back. Ready?"

But nothing happened, though he tried several times, and

nothing happened either when he went over to the arm exercises Lena showed him how to do, telling Grandad to touch his nose or his ear, or to open and close his fingers, and so on, and then doing it for him when he didn't respond. After a while Lena told him to stop even telling him, and just move the arm and hand around in different ways for five minutes, and do the same thing all over again on the other side, though he really couldn't expect any response there for a long while yet. She watched him for a bit, and then crossed to the other side of the ward and started working on one of the patients there, though she still glanced across from time to time.

When he thought he'd done enough he straightened up and looked round at her, and she nodded and made a gesture with her hands to tell him he could stop. He felt surprisingly tired, and it was a relief to sit down and read Grandad his e-mails.

Apart from Dad coming home for one weekend, that was the last good thing that happened for almost a month.

# 7

Nothing much bad happened in that month either. Except that *nothing* happened, and that was bad. It made it harder and harder to keep hoping, while everyone else was starting to give up. As the days went by Gavin began to imagine he could hear in everyone's voices—the nurses' and Mum's, even Gran's—that they were beginning to stop hoping.

On the day after Gavin had talked to Lena, Robert picked him up after school again and drove him to Aberdeen. He went straight up to the stroke unit. Lena was already in the ward, working on one of the other patients. She looked up, nodded, and smiled, so he settled himself in beside Grandad's bed. Grandad's right hand still wasn't fidgeting around, which was a relief. Gavin didn't start off by holding it, the way he'd always done before, because he wanted Lena to be there to see if anything happened when he did.

He'd got two new e-mails to read, one of them a three-pager from a model maker in Valparaiso whose English was only just good enough for the job. Usually Gavin would have found it fun making sense of it, but today it was difficult to concentrate enough. He felt desperately tense and nervous. All this was so important, and time never stopped leaking away, moment after moment after moment, and any of them might have been the one good moment when he could have got his message through to Grandad. He had to force himself to get up slowly and not leap eagerly to his feet when Lena stopped what she was doing and came over.

"Ready to try again, then?"

"I was just waiting for you. Do you want me to start straight in?"

"Might as well. I've been working with him already. I just left his arms for you to do."

Gavin put the e-mails away and positioned himself beside the bed, feeling tenser than ever. This wasn't a test, for heaven's sake, he told himself. Lena wasn't going to yell at him if he got something wrong, but still it really mattered in ways he didn't understand. Except that anything he did for Grandad *might* matter. He took a deep, steadying breath and positioned Grandad's arm so that he could hold his hand comfortably.

"Lena's here now, Grandad," he said, "and she's going to watch me doing your exercises with you. First off I'm going to grab hold of your hand and give it a bit of a squeeze . . . there. Feel that? Squeeze back if you felt it. . . ."

Nothing. Grandad's eyes were open, but his hand stayed fast asleep. Gavin had told himself, several times, this might happen, and managed to keep his voice cheerful.

"Never mind. I'll do it for you, to remind you."

Gently, with his free hand, he bent the sleeping fingers up. They didn't help. Didn't resist. Those tough, workman's fingers—Grandad used to crack walnuts with them, he'd once told Gavin; and they'd tied the tiny, precise knots and splices in *Selkie*'s sails and rigging. Don't think about that now. Leave it. Go on to the exercises. Somehow he kept his voice even, cheerful, as he moved Grandad's arm about, telling him what

60

he was going to do and encouraging him to help. Every now and then Lena stopped him and took over, but made him put his fingertips on the separate muscles so that he could feel how they stretched or bunched as she flexed the joints and twisted the hand to and fro. He could tell the difference at once when she moved round to the other arm and did the same things there, though he couldn't think of a way of describing it.

"The connections are still all there on his right side," Lena explained. "Only he can't remember how to use them. A lot of what we're trying to do is simply reminding him, and in a few days' time he should be starting to remember. It's different on his left side. A lot of the connections are broken there, and he's going to have to find new ones. That'll take a good bit longer, of course.

"Want to take over? Time I was moving on, in any case. Carry on on this side for another ten minutes, and then go back and do a bit more on his right. Don't overdo it. He'll be getting tired soon, and so will you, I daresay. We don't want to wear you out."

She was right. Doing the exercises wasn't that hard work, but it was boring, and surprisingly tiring. Boring because it was doing the same thing over and over, with no result, and tiring because it mattered so much. Time somehow stuck. That first ten minutes seemed to take forever. He sighed with relief when he could go round to the other side of the bed and finish doing the right arm.

This was just as tiring, but less dreary, because now he could really feel the difference, feel Grandad there, inside his sleeping arm, and from that go on to think that the pressure inside himself might perhaps have a purpose, that if he could somehow gather and shape it and find exactly the right place and moment, something might at last force its way through, and reach Grandad, and wake him from his sleep.

"That's enough, Grandad," he whispered at last. "Now let's have a bit of a rest."

He switched Grandad's hand into his own left hand so that he could sit, still holding it, and close his eyes and empty his mind and think about nothing at all, utterly exhausted, body and mind. The certainty, the self-assurance, that he'd begun to feel while he was doing the exercises, dwindled away. He'd hardly done anything, for heaven's sake—talked to Grandad a bit, moved his arms and fingers about a bit. There was no reason why he should have felt as tired as if he'd played a full game of football on a muddy field and then done two hours' difficult homework.

Right, so he was building up some kind of special magical power inside himself, which he was going to use to make Grandad well again? Like the selkies had given Grandad his stroke, because he'd been joking about them? Oh, yeah? Grandad had been going to have his stroke anyway. The GP's notes had come through, Mum said. Donald had been right— Grandad had had a couple of blackouts and been to Dr. Moray about them.

I've got to stop thinking like this, he told himself, and picked up *Model Boats* and opened it and started reading Grandad the first bit he came to. When he was bored with that he started on his homework, feeling buzzy and stupid, making a lot of mistakes and finding it difficult to think of anything worth saying to Grandad about it. Gran showed up when he was about halfway through so he moved himself out to a chair by the reception desk so that she could be alone with Grandad. He kept dozing off and had only just finished the homework when Lena looked in to say good-bye.

"Same time tomorrow?" he said.

"Not sure," she said slowly, frowning at him in a bothered kind of way. "Well, maybe. I'll call your mother. I'll get the number at the desk."

"Suppose you aren't here, do I . . . ?"

"No, leave it. Time I did a bit of work myself. See you soon."

She left, and he tried to go back to his homework but fell asleep again, and didn't remember anything about what happened after that, until he woke up in the car and saw they were back in Stonehaven, just turning up out of Slug Road.

Next morning, while he was stacking his dirties together to put in the dishwasher, Mum said, "Don't get up for a minute, darling. I need to talk to you."

She'd never been any good at hiding her feelings. He could always tell. This time, even before he looked at her, he knew it was something serious and he wasn't going to like it. He waited.

"Your friend Lena called last night," she said. "I'm sorry, darling, but she doesn't think you should go over to the hospital every day, and nor do I."

"Oh, Mum! But—"

"No, listen, darling. I was really thankful she called, because I was going to tell you the same off my own bat, but I knew you'd take it better from her. She's got a lot of experience, not just with stroke victims but with their families. She knows what a strain it is for them. She knows how helpless we all feel."

"But I don't feel helpless, Mum. Not while I'm *doing* something. I only will if you stop me."

"Yes, of course, darling. That's why Lena was so ready to let you do what you're doing. She thought it would also help you, just to feel that you were doing something for Grandad, but now she's beginning to wish she hadn't. You're putting too much strain on yourself. Already you're wearing yourself out. You won't last a week the way you're going, she says. And I agree."

"But, Mum . . . !"

"No, darling. You yourself know it's true. You were dead on your feet by the time I got to the ward last night. I had to steer you back to the car—you'd never have made it on your own. Grandad himself would tell you the same, and he'd tell you too that you've simply got to have a life of your own, doing the usual sort of things you do, hanging out with your friends, all that. . . ."

"It won't be any good, Mum. I won't be able to think about anything else. I'd be a complete drag."

"Well, you're going to have to try, darling. That's the deal. You can go on going to the hospital every other day, but only provided you promise me that you'll do your utmost best on your off days to lead an ordinary kind of life, like I said. If you can't promise me that, then I'll ask Robert to stop taking you over. You understand?"

She paused for an answer. Gavin could only stare at the table, shaking his head.

"It isn't all down to you, darling," she said quietly, laying her hand on his. "Really it isn't. That's very important. This is a team effort. We've all got to face the fact that Grandad may not get better, and if he doesn't it won't be anyone's fault. But if you keep thinking it's all down to you, then you're going to blame yourself for the rest of your life for letting it happen. That's why Lena and I have agreed to let you go over at all, so that you know in your heart you've done everything you possibly can.

"So next week you can go to the hospital every other day, and then we'll see how you're bearing up. All right? Now I'm going to call Robert and tell him he's let off taking you today. Poor man. Do you realize what he's given up for you out of Christian charity? He isn't allowed to smoke in the dispensary, of course, so the drive over to Aberdeen is his last chance of a decent drag on his disgusting cigarettes until whenever he has his coffee break. Who'd have imagined I'd ever feel any sympathy for a chain-smoker! You live and learn."

"All right," said Gavin slowly. "We'll give it a go. I'll do supper tonight. Is it okay if I don't go round to Mrs. McCracken's after school and go fishing instead? Leave me some money in case I don't catch anything."

"Well . . ."

Mum didn't really like him going about on his own, but she was better about it than some of the other mums.

"I'll take Dodgem to guard me," he suggested.

It was just a joke, to make it easier for her. You couldn't have imagined Dodgem guarding anything except his own dinner bowl.

"I'll go round to Brian's next time. He's got a new game."

"Oh, all right. Sugar snaps if they've got them. Give me a call when you're in."

It worked out okay. Thinking about it while he got himself ready for school, Gavin realized that he was actually relieved not to be going to the hospital every day. He didn't really *want* to—he'd just felt he *had* to, so he couldn't even have chosen not to. He'd needed Mum to stop him. Now, since he'd promised her, he'd do his best to keep his side of the bargain, and that meant, as far as possible, never being alone with time to start brooding, but really concentrating on his lessons, and mucking in with some of the others in whatever they were doing in break and so on.

He took a look at his homework on the way to school. He'd done the math first, and it was pretty awful, but the French was a disaster. Luckily it wasn't due till the afternoon, and he didn't want Miss Finch letting him off because of Grandad, so he did it again during dinner. He had a few bad patches during the day, but he shook them off. Literally. At one point he found himself deliberately giving his whole body a violent shudder as he tried to get rid of a mental image of Grandad lying in his bed in the ward.

Like Dodgem after he's been in the sea, he thought. Okay, I *will* take Dodgem fishing. Then we can walk along the beach to Safeway. He'll like that.

That worked out too, though he'd been afraid fishing hadn't been such a bright idea because it would give him plenty of time to brood. But getting Dodgem past all his message posts on the way down to the harbor was a bit of a distraction. Once there he flopped down onto the cobbles and went to sleep, and didn't even wake up while Gavin was heaving him, one end at a time, out of everyone's way.

It was a good day for fishing, mild and cloudy, and judging by the seagulls there were enough food scraps in the water to bring the mackerel in as well as the gulls. He landed a medium-sized one after a dozen casts.

At that point Tacky Steward showed up, and immediately came over to sympathize about Grandad. Gavin told him what was happening—easily, as if it were something that had happened to someone else—while he went on fishing, and before Tacky could get round to teaching him the best way to catch mackerel he hooked into another one. That gave Tacky the chance to advise him how to land it, and say, "That's the idea. Well done," as if it hadn't all been obvious stuff that Gavin had only just done with the first fish. Tacky was obviously set to go on like that all afternoon. Gran had a tiny appetite, and two good fish was quite enough for the three of them, with a bit to spare for Dodgem, so as soon as he'd landed the second one Gavin started to put his tackle away and Tacky had to go back to his own end of the wall and wait for someone else to show off to.

Dodgem actually came half awake on the beach. It was full of fascinating smells, and shallows to waddle in and out of, and then shake himself off, preferably over some sunbather or a passing jogger. Gran didn't take him there nearly often enough. She preferred the town center, because she met more people there. Donald had once calculated that what with her stopping to chat and Dodgem stopping to read and reply to his pee-mail they averaged a bit under half a mile an hour on their walks.

Gavin let him off his lead for a bit and mooched along, look-ing for smooth flat stones to play ducks and drakes with. The sea was calm enough for that, and he did a couple of twelve-skip throws—fifteen was his best ever. Then he put Dodgem back on his lead, hauled him along to Safeway, and left him behind the trolleys to guard the fishing gear in his sleep. He bought the sugar snaps, and bacon for Sunday breakfast, and three individual butterscotch-and-custard desserts, which Mum loved but never bought for herself because they were full of weird-sounding chemicals. If you bought one for her she ate it, because "it would have been wicked to waste it." Then he coaxed and lugged and bullied Dodgem back up to Arduthie Road.

Despite his having caught the fish so easily, it had all taken longer than he expected. He was turning the fish over to grill on the other side when he heard Mum's key in the door. He

put the sugar snaps on to steam, set the timer for three minutes, and opened the kitchen door.

"That smells good," she called. "I won't be a moment. How
did you get on?"

"Okay," he called back.

He'd probably have said that anyway, but it was true. It had
been an okay day. Something he'd really needed without
knowing it. Ordinary.

# 8

That was Friday. Saturday morning was swimming lessons down at the Leisure Center, which Mr. Tweedie had coaxed him into signing up for at the start of term, and Mum and Grandad had said was a good idea. Saturdays are a busy time for estate agents, but Mum had got Elsie and Bob to stand in for her and drove the three of them up to Aberdeen. She left Gran and Gavin at the hospital entrance and went off to do her shopping.

Several of the other patients had visitors, which would have made it awkward to do the exercises anyway, so Gavin simply settled on the other side of the bed and half listened to Gran's chat while he did the easy bits of homework. Her stories seemed really lively and interesting and amusing that day. He guessed she was making a special effort for Grandad. He'd never have known how sad she was inside if it hadn't been for what she'd told him at the hospital that time.

When she went off to chat with the nurse on duty—a new one Gavin hadn't met—he held Grandad's hand and told him, slowly, spinning it out with pauses, about fishing the day before, and Tacky wanting to teach him how to do it. Then he settled back to his homework, saying something about it every now and then, as usual, until Gran came back. When Mum arrived she talked to the nurse about how Grandad was getting on and what would happen next, and then came and told him about it, doing her best, but it wasn't her kind of thing. She liked stuff to happen when she spoke. Nothing happened with Grandad. After a while she took them home.

After supper he called Brian about coming round to look at his computer game the next day, and then watched TV with Gran. He wasn't that keen on the programs she liked, but she needed somebody there so she could tell them what she thought about everyone in the soaps, and he was feeling a bit ashamed about the way he'd been behaving and thinking, as if he were the only one Grandad truly mattered to, the only one who really cared. For the same reason he went to church with her next morning, which he didn't most Sundays, though Grandad usually did. Gavin didn't know what to think about church, and Grandad wouldn't tell him. "Got to make up your own mind," he said. "Only not yet." Mum believed in earth spirits and stuff, so she stayed home and cooked Sunday dinner.

After that he went round to Brian's. Brian's dad was in computers, so he had a lot of cast-off kit that still worked okay. The game was called Spec Ops, which stood for Special Operations, and two of you could play it on separate PCs, working together to shoot up the baddies. Brian had had plenty of practice, but Gavin picked it up soon enough and they had a good time until Brian's dad came and shooed them out into the open air for a bit of exercise. They took their bikes up into Dunnottar woods the other side of the stream and joined Terry and Tony and a couple of others whooping round the mountain-bike track in the old quarry. Gavin came off into a bramble and cut his arm. It bled a bit, but he licked it clean and got home tired enough and hungry enough to feel he'd had a really good time.

Another okay, ordinary day.

The first Monday after the change he got to the stroke unit telling himself, Okay. Mum's right. There's no point in my wearing myself stupid trying to get through to Grandad by some sort of crazy magic pressure inside me that nobody else can do. Who do I think I am? Harry Potter? It isn't all down to me, and anyway I'll be much more use to him if I do it the sensible way, and forget about the selkies and all that.

But it didn't work out like that.

Lena wasn't in the ward, and he decided he'd better not start in on the exercises without her say-so, so he just took hold of Grandad's hand, as usual, and started to tell him, a bit at a time, about the new system, and what Mum had said, and why she'd been right really, and it was crazy of him to think the selkies had anything to do with it. But almost at once his voice started to choke up, because it all mattered far, far too much for him to control, and he realized that the pressure was back, worse than it had ever been, and there wasn't anything he could do about it.

He stopped talking and simply waited until he thought he could speak normally again, provided it was about something else, like the e-mails or Tacky or school. It was only then that he felt something pressing against the side of his palm, and looked down and saw that Grandad was holding his hand again.

He'd no idea how long he'd been doing that for, and now, as he stood staring, Grandad gave a gentle sigh and let go.

He told Lena when she came, and she was interested and puzzled, but he didn't try to make it happen again. He was pretty sure it wasn't any use. And nothing like that happened when he went on to do the exercises. He didn't get any response at all, and he was just as tired as ever when he finished.

But thinking about it on his way home in the car, he decided that was a sort of private message, for him alone, and what it told him was that though Mum had been right, and getting Grandad well wasn't all down to him alone, there still *was* something that only he could do, and no one else. He didn't know what it was yet, but it was something to do with the pressure inside him, and he'd been wrong to try and stop it. What he'd got to do was let it happen, and find out about it, and then, in the end, he'd be able to use it.

So for the next three weeks Gavin's life fell into two halves. He felt almost as if he'd become two different people. Tuesdays, Thursdays, and weekends he was Stonehaven Gavin and Mondays, Wednesdays, and Fridays he was hospital Gavin.

Hospital Gavin felt utterly different from the normal, Stonehaven Gavin. The moment he woke, all through breakfast and school, he could feel the pressure beginning to build. He nursed it, looked after it, let it happen unseen inside him. He didn't think about it all the time, did his work okay, talked with the other kids, and so on, but he didn't waste any energy getting involved. His friends might have noticed he was a bit quieter those days, but they probably didn't.

Then the bell went, and he gathered his things, and Robert was waiting in his car out in the road, and they drove up to Aberdeen. Lena was usually in the ward. Some days she watched him for a while; mostly she just said hello and left him to it.

He said hi to Grandad, sorted his stuff out, talked, or read to him if he'd got anything to read, and then started on the exercises.

Now the sense of pressure reversed as he tried to pour everything that was in him, his whole soul, all that gathered strength and need, into the slow, monotonous exercises.

"Now, Grandad, see if you can touch your nose."

Count slowly to six. Adjust arm. Grip wrist and elbow. Raise forearm. Shift grip. Uncurl forefinger. Lower arm and hand to touch nose.

"Great. Now you can put it down again."

Count slowly to six. . . .

There was never even a flicker of response, apart from the slow lopsided blink every so often, and it wasn't Grandad doing that, really. It was just something that happened. There was never even the slightest glimmer in the vague blue stare. It was as if the selkie had gone from the harbor and mightn't ever come back.

The image haunted him. On the Saturday morning Dad was home Gavin took him down to fish for mackerel, and between them they caught enough to spare one for a seal, if it had appeared, but it didn't. Dad was obviously having a great time—he used to fish with Grandad years ago, he said, whenever Grandad was home from *his* ship—so Gavin was careful

74

not to let him see how he was feeling. He knew it was stupid, but he'd really longed for the seal to appear and look at him the way it had that first day, and it hadn't. Why should it? Magic doesn't work in the real world.

As the days went by he got to know the nurses. They were very kind to him. When there wasn't anyone else in the ward they treated him almost like one of themselves, as if he was part of Grandad's treatment, which he was, sort of. They took him out into their office for a cup of tea when the shifts changed and they were all in the ward together. The tea trolley didn't come round the stroke unit on weekdays because it wasn't any use to the patients there. They let him draw the curtains a little way along the bed so that he could be more alone with Grandad, and Angie found a high stool he could sit on so that Grandad could see his face, supposing he was seeing anything.

There were four of them: Angie, who was Scottish, and three foreign ones, Duli from Thailand, Janet from New Zealand, and Véronique, who he'd met before. She was French, but she wasn't just working here for a couple of years, like the other two. She was married to a Scotsman, an airline pilot, so now she lived in Aberdeen while he flew all round the world. She showed him a picture of her two daughters. They were twins, but they didn't look at all like each other.

"Everybody tell me one is Scottish and one is French," she said.

"Bet you they both talk better English than you do," said Angie, which Gavin thought was funny coming from her as she talked really broad Scots herself. He showed Grandad the photograph so that he could see what they were laughing about.

75

The ward sister was Sister Taylor. She was older than the others, hardly taller than Gavin, plump, with a pale round face and a very soft, even voice. There was something about the way she looked at him with her round gray eyes that made Gavin feel he had to be careful with her and not do anything she mightn't like. He wasn't exactly scared of her, but he guessed she could be very, very tough if she wanted to. From one or two things the nurses said, he could tell they felt the same.

The nurses never said anything to suggest Grandad wasn't going to get better, but after a while he began to notice that they never said anything either to suggest that he might. He was careful not to ask because it wouldn't have been fair. They'd have had to say yes, of course he might, even if they didn't believe it.

Lena was the only person who said anything directly. About three weeks after Grandad's stroke, Gavin was a bit late getting to the hospital because they'd been doing something to the Torry Bridge and it had taken Robert a while to get past the traffic lights. Lena was still in the ward and he could tell she'd been waiting for him.

"There's something I wanted to ask you," she said. "I've got a hunch that there's something a bit odd about Robbie's case. I've got almost nothing to go on, nothing I can show or explain to anyone else. The suddenness with which the ataxia stopped is a bit unusual, but apart from that there's only what I've got from you, only the two or three times your grandfather seemed to be deliberately holding your hand. I don't think you're making that up—I saw it happen once, but there's no denying that he's made very little progress since those first couple of days, and other people are going to say, 'Okay, it did happen then, but that might have been just a coincidence, and maybe the kid's persuading himself about the other times.' You see?

"But I still believe there's something there, and that's the only clue we've got. So let's go back to that first time. You were holding his hand and talking to him, and you said something that seemed to produce a moment of awareness in his eyes, and you think that's when it began."

"That's right."

"Can you remember what you were talking about? I'm clutching at straws, really, but I wonder if it mightn't possibly provide us with a clue."

"Er . . . well . . . Look, this is going to sound pretty stupid, but . . . You see, the day before Grandad's stroke we were fishing down at the harbor, fishing for mackerel, and . . ."

Stumbling and ashamed, because it felt like something stupid and private, he told her about the seal, and Grandad saying it might have been a selkie, and then about the boat Grandad was making for him, and deciding to call her *Selkie*, and Grandad saying he'd better go and ask the selkies if they minded—just one of Grandad's jokes, of course—and that being the moment Grandad had had his stroke. And then about getting back from the hospital and going down to the harbor next morning and saying sorry to the selkies and asking them for permission.

"So that's what I was telling him I'd done," he said, "when . . . when I saw his eyes change."

This time he managed not to cry, just.

"Something to do with the boat, do you think?" said Lena, frowning.

"I've told him about her quite a bit. She wasn't quite finished, you see, so I've been doing that, and it was something to tell him—I knew he'd be interested. I've finished now, except for the name—I don't seem ever to get the stencils neat enough. But . . . Lena, we've only got a week left, haven't we?"

"What do you mean?"

"Don says you'll give Grandad a month and then make up your minds how he's doing and if you decide he hasn't got any better you'll move him out to the Kincardine or somewhere. And he isn't, is he?"

Lena sighed.

"That's what I was talking to the consultant about. I still in my heart of hearts believe that we could get through, if only we could find the key—just get *in*, somehow, and stimulate him to try and get himself out—he's the only person who can do that, but he doesn't realize because he can't understand what's happening to him. The consultant is sympathetic, and there's been a bit of a lull for once, but it looks like that's over, and he's got other patients to think about. He can't keep your grandfather on here just because I've got a hunch about him. But if I could show him some definite sign—it's got to be more than a gleam in the eyes or a twitch—a voluntary movement perhaps, a response to something I've said or you've said—then he'd have an excuse to say, 'Yes, we'll keep him on for a bit.' You see?"

"Yes, but . . . Well, what about . . . ? Oh, I don't know. . . ."

Lena smiled.

"Like I said, we're clutching at straws," she said.

Gavin nodded. What he wanted to try was certainly that.

That evening, after supper, he climbed wearily up to the attic to have another go at cutting stencils for *Selkie*'s name. He'd started trying as soon as he'd finished the stand. He needed three stencils, two with just the name for the bow, so that he didn't have to reuse one, and a third one for the stern, with the home port, Stonehaven, below it. Plus a couple of spares in case something went wrong. That meant that all the "Selkie"s had to be exactly the same. It shouldn't have been too difficult, using one of Grandad's tiny, sharp knives, as there were no completely separate bits in any of the letters of the main name, and only the "O" and the "A" in "Stonehaven." He could leave little bridges of paper to hold those two in place and paint over the gaps by hand when he took the stencils away.

Usually he was pretty good at this sort of thing, but even on ordinary, Stonehaven-Gavin days, when he wasn't worn out from visiting Grandad, he kept making botch after botch. He'd no idea why, except perhaps he was really caring too much, but with a tiny corner of his mind he half believed that the selkies didn't want him to name the boat after them—though he called her *Selkie* whenever he talked or thought about her—because they hadn't yet given him permission. Anyway, he hadn't even tried for the last few days. The evenings were getting longer, so he'd taken Dodgem down to the beach instead.

Now, though, it had got to be done, somehow. The straw he was clutching at was that he would take the boat over to the hospital on his birthday so that Grandad could hold it in his hands and give it to him. If that was going to work either way—in Lena's world or the selkies'—*Selkie* had to be *finished*. He didn't know how he knew that, but he did.

This time the stencils went better. He still made mistakes, and threw away twice as many as he kept, and after forty minutes' intense concentration his eyes were weeping and his fingers became clumsy and stupid and he had to give up. So it took him three evenings, which left five more before his birthday. He'd already painted a bit of spare wood the right hull color, so he spent most of the first one practicing with some of the stencils that he hadn't got quite right. When he'd worked out just how thick the paint had to be, and how much to put on, and which brush to use, and so on, and then decided he'd got as good as he was ever going to, he taped his three best stencils in place, tidied up, and went to bed.

Next evening, working very carefully, he painted the names in and left them to dry while he caught up with Grandad's e-mails. Then he painted in the gaps on the "O" and "A," certain that at this very last minute he'd make a splodge and there wouldn't be time to paint it over and try again, but he didn't. With a sigh of relief he cleaned the brush, tidied the workbench, moved the small round table to the middle of the room, put a blue cloth over it, and set *Selkie,* on her stand, in the middle of it. He arranged the lights the way he'd seen Grandad

80

do when he'd finished a model and was ready to photograph it. Grandad had shown him how to use his camera, and he took a whole spool.

That was Friday evening. His birthday wasn't till Wednesday, but Véronique would be on duty on Sunday, and he wanted to show the photographs to her as well as to Grandad. She'd been interested in *Selkie* in the first place, and she usually asked how he was getting on, and she was very good at managing Sister Taylor.

That was important, because there was this . . . this feeling Gavin had—it didn't make sense—he wouldn't have wanted to tell anyone else about it, just as he hadn't wanted to tell Lena when it had first come to him. It had been weaker then, but more and more, while he'd been working on the stencils, he'd begun to believe that this was their last chance—that everything depended on the moment when he would put *Selkie* into Grandad's hands, so that they were both holding her, together. This was going to be the moment and the place for which he'd been waiting. *Selkie* was going to become a kind of bridge between them, a channel, a way for the buildup of pressure to break through and reach in to Grandad and wake him from his long sleep. So he didn't want anyone who knew Grandad in ordinary kinds of ways, like Mum or Gran, coming in and taking over and *talking* about her.

He knew this feeling was silly—crazy, even—but it was very strong.

# 9

Gavin left Mum and Gran talking across Grandad's bed, and
followed Véronique out of the ward when she went to make
herself a cup of tea in the tiny kitchen behind the office. She
looked at the photos one by one.

"Oh, but she is beautiful!" she whispered. "He make this for
you?"

"It took him four months. He only makes two or three a year,
and mostly he sells them for quite a lot of money, but *Selkie*'s for
me, for my birthday. It's on Wednesday. I got her finished just in
time. . . . Véronique, do you think I could bring her in with me
on Wednesday, so that Grandad can give her to me himself?"

"Why not? I must ask Sister, but of course she say yes when
I show her the photographs. You leave me this one, and this
one? She is here tomorrow. She tell you then."

"Great. Thanks a lot. And don't say anything to Mum about
it now. She'd just start making plans."

"Understood. My mother too is like this."

That evening Gavin rang Robert on Grandad's extension
and asked if it would be all right to pick him up from home on
Wednesday, a few minutes later than usual, as there was something he needed to take over to the hospital. Robert said fine.
He did this on sports days anyway, when Gavin had kit he
didn't want to ferry back and forth to Aberdeen, so he knew it
was okay with Mum.

On Monday Sister Taylor gave him the photographs back.

"You want to bring the boat over so that he can give it to you himself, Véronique tells me," she said.

"If that's all right."

"I don't see why not. He's perfectly stable. We'll move him into the single-bed ward for the day, provided nobody comes in suddenly. You'd like to be alone together a wee while?"

"Oh, yes, please! That'd be terrific."

"When I was little my gran looked after me because my ma went out to work. She was the most important person in my life. Then she got ill and I used to get taken to see her in hospital. It's why I went into nursing, really."

"Did she get better?"

"It wasn't the sort of thing you get better from. Mind you, it took her a wee while to die still."

Gavin felt himself go cold. A few evenings ago, when he'd gone downstairs to say good night, Gran had been watching the TV, or rather channel-surfing for something she might want to watch. For a moment she'd clicked onto a program about old people who get sick and *aren't* going to get better—there'd been this long, bleak room, these two rows of beds, these shapes in the beds. . . . Now he had a sudden picture in his mind of a plump, pale little girl who watched everything that was going on around her and never said much about it and never told anyone else what she was thinking or feeling. In the picture she was standing beside a bed looking at somebody she loved more than anyone else in the world. The bed was in a place like the one he'd seen on the TV. A people dump, the man had called it. Even if they took Grandad to the

Kincardine, that was where he'd be going really. To a people dump.

On Wednesday they got up early, and all three had breakfast together while Gavin opened his family presents. (His official birthday party with his friends was going to be down at the Leisure Center on Saturday.) Mum, rather surprisingly, had come up with a mobile phone.

"For you to keep in touch now you're beginning to gad about on your own," she explained, laughing.

And Gran, bless her heart, had come up with a set of modeler's carving tools, nestling in their own special box. She had a good time telling him who she'd consulted down at the hardware store to make sure she got the best ones, which you wouldn't have found in ordinary shops. That gave Gavin time to pull himself together and thank her properly. A month ago he'd have been thrilled with them, but what was the point now, without Grandad?

"Aren't you going to bring *Selkie* down too?" said Mum.

"I'm taking her over to Aberdeen, so Grandad can give her to me himself," he said. "Robert's picking me up here, so I don't have to take her in to school. I didn't want to bother you."

Mum blinked.

"High time you had that phone, obviously," she said, and laughed again. He realized that she understood quite well why he wanted to make his own arrangements. Some of it, anyway.

Just as Sister Taylor had promised, Grandad was in a small, separate ward. Angie showed him in and left. There were two beds, one pushed against the wall and the other one with Grandad in it. Gavin guessed that the nurses must simply have wheeled Grandad through in his own bed and shoved the other one out of the way. There was a card on the bedside table saying "Happy Birthday, Gavin." All four nurses had signed it, and someone else called Enid. It took him a moment to realize that this must be Sister Taylor.

He put *Selkie* and his satchel and stuff down on the floor and turned to the bed. The nurses shifted Grandad's body around during the day, to stop him getting bedsores, but by the time Gavin came Lena had usually left him lying on his back, with his head propped on pillows and both arms out on the counterpane, ready for the exercises. Gavin rearranged them on the central hummock of the body, with the hands close together, palms upward, and stuffed the bedclothes up under the elbows to hold them in place. They came loosely, without any resistance. It struck him how much thinner and lighter they seemed than when he'd first started helping Grandad do his exercises.

When he was ready he turned and picked up *Selkie* from her stand.

"Hi, Grandad," he said. "How's things? Look, I've brought *Selkie* for you to give me. I managed to get her finished. The names were a bit of a fiddle, but I did them with stencils. I hope you think they're good enough. Isn't she absolutely beautiful?"

Leaning over the bed and twisting his body sideways, he carefully lowered *Selkie* between Grandad's hands, with her keel resting on his body, then, one hand at a time, let go and lifted Grandad's hands and held them against the hull, so that Grandad was holding *Selkie* with Gavin's help. It was an incredibly awkward posture but he stuck it out as long as he could.

Nothing happened, nothing at all. Gavin didn't know what he'd expected—some change, some twitch, some *answer*. Nothing. Only the same, unfaltering feel of the backs of Grandad's hands against his fingers and palms, one not alive, not dead; one just sleeping. When every joint and muscle in his body seemed to be screaming at him to move he gave up, eased Grandad's hands free, and straightened up, cradling *Selkie* against his chest.

"Thank you so much," he whispered. "I think she's the most beautiful boat anyone ever made."

He stood for several minutes by the bed, cradling *Selkie* in his hands. No, he thought, this was the wrong way. I got it upside down. There's been just three times since Grandad's stroke when anyone's got through to him, and each time it's been me, and he held my hand to tell me. And each time I'd been saying something about the selkies. It isn't *Selkie* that really matters, not that way—it's the selkies. But I was right about *Selkie* being a sort of bridge. Not to Grandad, though. To them . . . Yes . . .

Slowly he settled *Selkie* back on her stand, pulled his stool up to the bed, and started to read Grandad his e-mails.

The nurses left him alone a long while. He'd almost finished his homework before Angie poked her head round the door.

"Can we come in now?" she said. "We're just going off."

"Yes, of course. Mum and Gran will be here soon anyway."

Angie opened the door wide and held it for Janet to come marching through, proudly bearing a small chocolate cake with eleven lit candles on it, as if she were carrying the boar's head into a king's banquet. Véronique and Duli followed her.

"Sister's keeping an eye on the ward," Angie explained. "And Janet made the cake, so you'd better tell her it's wonderful."

Gavin didn't know what to say. His feelings seemed to be all muddled up. It was really nice of them, but it wasn't what he wanted, and he couldn't tell them that. He managed to stammer thank-yous, and blow the candles out, and make his face smile, and tell Janet the cake was really wicked, which it was, and save pieces for Gran and Mum and a bit for Gran to give to Dodgem—all that—and go on doing that sort of thing when Mum and Gran showed up, and no one seemed to notice anything was wrong, but when they all left and he went to say thank you to Sister Taylor for letting it happen, and show her *Selkie*, he thought he could tell, just from the way she looked at him, that she understood some of what he might be feeling. Not all of it. Nobody could know or guess that.

Mum had got Gavin's favorite pizza for supper, but he could hardly eat a mouthful. He felt empty, meaningless, useless, utterly exhausted, body and soul, and went to bed early, though he was certain he was hardly going to sleep at all. How could he, knowing what he was going to have to do before he next went to see Grandad, the day after the next?

# 10

Ⅰn fact he fell asleep almost at once and slept without dreams and woke at the usual time to face a Stonehaven day. He'd been tempted to do the thing at once, to get it over, but he decided to give himself this ordinary, no-pressure day to make certain that he still knew for sure that he'd got to do it.

He'd become pretty good at not thinking about Grandad on Stonehaven days, but this was different. He positively wanted to have his idea at the back of his mind all the time, as if he were testing it against the ordinariness of the world he knew, school, and meals, and messing around with Garry and Ian and the others. There were times when it surged up and almost overwhelmed him, until he nearly decided he couldn't bear to do it, but in the end it stood the test and he went to bed with his mind made up.

The alarm went off under his pillow at half past four. He lay and listened. Mum's light snore was still coming steadily from her room next door. Gran's room was upstairs, where she wasn't so likely to hear anything. Carefully he slid out of bed.

He'd laid all his clothes ready and left the door slightly ajar, wedging it in place with a T-shirt so that he could open it without the lock rattling. When he was dressed he put *Selkie* under his arm and crept down the stairs in his socks. The inner door clicked slightly. Holding his breath, he stood and listened. Mum's snore had faltered, stopped. Very carefully he let out his breath and waited. Silence, no rustle of a duvet being moved aside, no call. He slipped through the door and managed to close it without a click.

They all kept their wellies in the little lobby. He slid his on and put *Selkie* down on her side so that he had two hands free and could stop the security chain from clanking when he unfastened it. This lock clicked slightly too when he opened the door, and again when he closed it behind him, but he didn't think Mum would hear with the other one shut.

Summer nights had begun to get very short this far north, so it was already bright day, though the sun wouldn't be up for a bit yet. If anybody saw him he was ready to explain that he was taking his new boat down to the bay to see how she sailed, before he had to get ready for school, but he'd much rather not talk to anyone, so he turned down the alley just beyond the hotel to avoid the main street. An early jogger passed him in Slug Road, but barely glanced at him.

There were a few strollers, as well as the joggers, out on the seafront promenade, so before crossing it he waited till nobody was near enough to notice how beautiful *Selkie* was, and to want to talk about her. But once he was down the steps and onto the beach there was no one else about. The tide was well out, with light waves lapping against the shingle, and a gentle offshore breeze blowing, just as he would have expected with the sea warmer than the land after the cooling night.

He waded into the water far enough for the keel to clear in the troughs between the light waves, set *Selkie* afloat, and adjusted the sails and rudder. Deliberately he'd left the radio control box behind in case at the last minute he couldn't bear it and changed his mind.

When he was satisfied with the setting he turned his head seaward and called out in a strong voice, "This is for you, selkie. It's the most precious thing I can give you. Please, please help me get Grandad back."

Then he let go for the last time.

She faltered slightly as she nosed into the next line of foam, rose to it, and sailed smoothly on. She sailed like a dream over the pearly gray dawn sea, rising and falling steadily to the rhythm of the waves. He watched her out of sight and walked slowly back up the hill, telling himself that this was the last, most desperate thing he could try. It filled him with a terrible bitter ache of loss, but he'd had to do it. If it didn't work, then nothing else would.

He dragged himself home long before breakfast-time, but he couldn't face eating so he just dirtied a bowl with a bit of milk and cornflakes because Mum was bound to notice if he didn't. She noticed something all the same, and asked him if he was all right.

"I'm fine," he said. "Just I'm not properly awake yet."

"No wonder. You're needing the sleep. Robert's taking you to the hospital after school, as usual?"

"Yes, of course. It's Friday."

"I'll try and be over by five-thirty. I want to talk to Sister."

Somehow he forced himself through school. He longed to go and hide in the library, like he had that first day after Grandad's stroke, but he knew that would only make it worse. Doing something—anything—helped him stop thinking about what he'd done. The utter, pointless loss, the stupidity, the certainty that soon Mum and Gran were going to notice, and ask, came flooding back into his mind, like vomit in the throat, and he had to gulp it down again. Luckily none of the teachers noticed, but some of the other kids did. He muttered furiously that he was okay and they left him alone. He ate only a couple of bites of his lunch sandwich and threw the rest in the bin.

When the bell rang he snatched up his stuff and shot out, barging through the scrum at the main door. Robert was waiting for him. After that he hardly noticed anything till he was pushing through the swing door into the stroke unit. At that point everything slowed down and became extraordinarily sharp and clear.

Janet was in the ward, with her back to the door, and didn't see him. Grandad's bed was back in its corner. No, it wasn't—it was a different bed with someone else in it.

They'd taken Grandad away. . . .

No, not yet. They were going to, this evening, and . . . the real reason why Mum was coming over early was so that she could be here when Sister told Gavin.

So Grandad would still be in the single-bed ward where they'd put him for Gavin's birthday.

He slipped quietly out and along the passage. Nobody saw him. Yes, Grandad was there.

This was the time, the place, the last chance for something to happen, like he seemed to have known all along it was going to be.

With a sigh of relief Gavin put his satchel down and pushed the door a bit shut, far enough to hide one side of the bed from anyone passing by. He wasn't supposed to do this, of course. He just hoped it looked as if it had happened by accident.

He fetched his stool, sat down, leaned over the bed, and took Grandad's hand, wrapping the sleeping fingers round his own as best he could, to make it feel something like really holding hands.

"Hi, Grandad," he said. "I'll read you your e-mail in a minute—there isn't that much—but there's something I've got to tell you first. . . ."

After the first few words his voice started to go funny and husky. He kept having to stop and get control of it. The hoarded pressure was building up inside him, trying to burst out. It all mattered so much, more than anything else in the world. This *had* to work. He *had* to believe in it to make it work. He *did* believe in it, almost. . . .

Behind him the door moved.

Slowly, not knowing what to expect, he turned.

It was only Janet.

"Hello, Gavin. Didn't know you'd showed up. How's things?"

"They're taking him away, aren't they? There's a new patient in his corner."

"Well . . . um . . . I'll tell Sister you're here—she's busy just now. . . . Don't you worry, Gavin. He'll still be looked after. He'll be fine."

It wasn't her fault. It wasn't anyone's fault. Gavin managed a sort-of smile.

"I'm just going to read him his e-mail," he said.

"Great," she said. "See you soon."

He turned back to Grandad, reached for the limp hand, and hesitated. The mood of almost-belief had been broken, and he was back to knowing in his heart that it was all nonsense.

Try again later, he thought, and got the e-mails out. There were only two of them, both short. He read them, and suggested how he might answer them, always finishing with a question ("That okay with you, Grandad? Right." Or something like that). Still nothing seemed to be happening inside him, so he started on his homework as usual, telling Grandad about it as he went along.

Time went by. The nurses changed shifts. Janet and Duli looked in to say good-bye, which they didn't normally bother with. It didn't matter. He still felt perfectly ordinary, apart from being hungry and wishing he hadn't binned his lunch. When he'd done his homework he read a few bits out of the new *Model Boats*. Nothing changed, only time seemed to be going faster than it had done all day, and he knew he'd just been putting off trying again. Gran wasn't coming today, but Mum would be here in half an hour. With a reluctant sigh he put everything back in his satchel and took Grandad's hand.

He started at the beginning, as if he'd just come into the room.

"Hi, Grandad . . ."

But it wasn't the same. The words came steadily, in his normal voice, almost as if he'd been talking about some other kid he'd watched wade into the sea and launch his model fishing-smack out on the morning breeze. He couldn't even make it interesting. He was just talking to himself because he knew Grandad couldn't hear him.

He stopped before he'd got to the end. It wasn't worth the misery of pretending.

And now it hit him. It was like a wave surging against a cliff. There was a particular cleft below the cliff path on the far side of Dunnottar Castle where sometimes just before high tide, even on an almost calm day, a slow, deep swell, something you could hardly see was a wave at all, would lurch against the cliff face, forcing itself into the cleft, and the sheer weight of the raised sea behind it would send a column of water roaring unstoppably up the cleft and shooting a glittering pillar of foam out into the sunlight above.

Like that. Inside him. The awfulness of what he'd done, the lovely boat gone, the boat Grandad had given him, made for him, spent the last months of his life on, lost, lost, thrown away . . .

He was really weeping now, gasping for breath between his sobs. . . .

"Oh, selkie, help me," he croaked as the tears streamed down his cheeks, down his nose. He licked them from his lips. They were salt, like the sea. . . .

"You wantin' something, young laddie?"

He looked up, but couldn't see, blinded by his own tears. He wiped his sleeve across his eyes, trying to clear them, but everything was still a blur, as if the room was filled with fog.

A shape loomed in the fog—somebody—who . . . ?

He wiped again and saw it must be one of the hospital tea ladies, judging by her apron and cap, though he couldn't see her trolley—everything was still a blur, apart from her head and shoulders. She had a pale, round face, round dark eyes, and two or three hairy warts on her top lip.

"I want my Grandad," he sobbed, like a small lost boy in a crowded market. "I want to talk to him."

She just stared at him as if he were the strangest thing she'd ever seen. He was crying again, the tears filling his eyes, blurring her out, but he heard her laugh, a sharp, yapping noise. There was a roaring in his ears, drowning the swish of the door and the rattle of her trolley, but he knew she'd gone.

He should have asked her for something to eat. He felt very peculiar, empty inside, hollow, like that time just before he'd fainted. He felt himself falling off the stool and tried to stand up, lost his balance, and staggered against the bed. Everything had gone muzzy, everything except Grandad's hand in his own hand. Desperately he clung to it as he tumbled across the bed.

The bed didn't stop his fall. It melted round him, melted into a sort of red mist. Or was it him melting, vanishing into the mist? He opened his mouth to cry out, and the tears dribbled into it, salt, like the sea, but there seemed to be no throat behind the mouth, nothing to cry out through, no lungs, nothing except the sea-taste, salt on his tongue, and the feel of Grandad's hand in his own.

And then even those were gone and there was nothing. Only a sort of bodiless Gavin-bubble, lost, helpless, floating in the roaring red mist.

# 11

Thud. *Thud. Thud.* Soft, booming thuds, endless, unchanging, going on and on through the roaring.

He'd been holding Grandad's hand. . . .

Where was Grandad's hand? He wanted to grope for it, but he couldn't, because his own hand wasn't there. It wasn't anywhere.

What had happened to his hand? To his other hand? *Him?*

The mist seemed to pulse with the thuds, and the Gavinbubble pulsed too because it was part of the mist, getting thicker and thinner as the mist pulsed, because the mist and the roaring were inside him as well as outside, a ghastly feeling. That was all there was of Gavin, a sort of feeling, floating lost in the mist. The feeling didn't have eyes to see the mist with, ears to hear the roaring with. It wasn't like that. The Gavin-feeling *was* the mist, it *was* the roaring, and they were all that Gavin was, all he would ever be, all he would ever know. . . .

No. Now something . . . What . . . ? Where . . . ?

Nowhere.

A yellow bucket in that nowhere, half full of filthy water. The water slopping about, starting to rise, slopping out over the edges, sluicing over the floor, rising, rising, a stupid little bit of green cloth to wipe it up with . . . horrible, horrible . . . he didn't know why . . .

Gone.

Red mist and roaring and thuds . . .

Voices . . . People talking close by. What are they saying? Can't hear through the thuds and the roaring. Call to them, shout for help!

Can't. No voice, nothing to shout with . . .

Gone.

Oh, please come back! Please!

Red mist and roaring and thuds . . .

Now something . . . somewhere . . . happening to someone . . .

Someone leaning on a bulwark at the side of a ship, looking out over an intensely dark blue sea. Heavy, slow waves under a clear pale sky. Between sky and sea, all along the horizon, a line of dazzling whiteness, brighter, whiter than the foam that rimmed the waves. Gavin knew, because the someone knew, what was being looked at. The whiteness was the floes and glaciers of the Antarctic, on the far side of the world.

Now the someone looked downward, and saw the greasy black side of the ship, with a great shape close against it, a shape heaving to the heave of the waves, pale on its near side, blue-black on its far side, and streaked across with scarlet as the blood pumped from three wounds, each made by a stocky harpoon that was stuck deep in the flesh of the dying whale. There was an open boat alongside the whale, men working cables round the immense body.

The someone was shaking his head. Gavin could feel two separate lots of feelings, the Gavin-thing-in-the-bubble's own shock and anguish at what was being done to the whale, and the someone's, which were grimmer and more complicated, revulsion and sorrow mixed in with anger and guilt.

Still looking at the whale, the someone spoke to the man beside him. The man laughed contemptuously. . . .

But before Gavin could grasp the moment, fix it, understand where it belonged and how he belonged with it, the mist came surging back, pulsing to the steady unending thuds, and once again they were all there was, all that Gavin Robinson was—the eyeless, earless, bodiless almost-nothing he had somehow become. . . .

It happened again and again and again. The mist dissolved, the roaring and the thuds ended, and there was a moment, a glimpse, an empty can, a broken gate, a dead bird in the gutter, meaningless things but somehow awful with loss or awful with disgust, loss and disgust that stayed like a taste in the mouth long after the red mist had swallowed the stupid things and swept them away.

And then, sometimes, something else, something that seemed to promise the beginnings of sense and meaning in the middle of the meaningless mess, but before he could grasp and use it to find out what was happening to him, it slipped away and there wasn't anything left to make sense of.

It wasn't always the dying whale, though that kept coming back, but so did the woman in the green dress walking on the shore at Stonehaven and talking over her shoulder to a kid behind her; only the kid wasn't listening because he'd stopped to try and drag a bit of old rope out of a pile of seaweed. Someone was watching her. The woman was Gran, but she wasn't, the way people are and aren't themselves in dreams sometimes, and Gavin wanted to call to her for help, but he hadn't got anything to call with. The someone wanted to call to her too, because he was fond of her and thought it was funny and typical that she should be talking away when there wasn't anyone to listen to her—Gavin could feel that on top of his own feelings—but before either of them could do anything the mist and the roaring and the thuds took over again.

And the same with everything else: nighttime, angry men yelling at each other, the gaudy bright lights of a bar behind them, the loom of a crane above them, black against huge bright stars; himself, Gavin, but only about six years old, pushing out through a gang of kids at the primary school door; a rough, dark sea crowded with ships all steaming in the same direction, the sense of tension and danger . . .

Each time Gavin knew what he was looking at, because the someone knew. The quarreling men had just come out of a bar in Singapore; Gavin had been coming out after his first day in a new school; the ships were a wartime convoy; and so on. And each time the moment of clarity brought with it a sudden flood of relief and hope, hope that now things would sort themselves out and that the someone could get back where he belonged, and Gavin could too. But then the roaring mist and the thuds surged back and wiped out even the memory of the moment, so that each time the same thing came again it seemed new, and brought the same relief and hope and understanding. When it was about small-Gavin coming out of school he knew that the someone was Grandad, no problem. But at the same time he knew that he, Gavin-now, was in desperate trouble but he couldn't remember what the trouble was, and for a moment he became small-Gavin and tried to lift up his arms and call out to Grandad to help him, but Gavin-now hadn't got any arms and small-Gavin just ran forward laughing. And then the roaring mist came back and he couldn't hang on to the knowledge, and so couldn't work out that yes, the woman in the green dress was Gran, and so the boy had to be Dad when he was about twelve. He didn't even remember about the someone there in the red mist with him until another moment came.

Only one thing didn't get forgotten. Each time the mist surged up it brought with it the understanding that all this had happened before, again and again and again, and it was going to go on like that forever. And with that knowledge came an awful wave of anger and despair and utter, utter boredom. That stayed. It was worse than the way the horror and loss lingered on after the stupid stuff that had brought them was gone. Much, much worse. It was like when you bite into an apple that's had a bug in it, and there's this foul bitter, corky taste, so you spit your mouthful out, but you can't get rid of the taste, however much you rinse your mouth out.

That was the worst thing, the despair, the utter boredom, the useless, frustrated rage at what was happening to him, and was going to go on happening, no end, no one to help him, no one ever. . . .

"Grandad," he groaned.

He had nothing to groan with. It was a groan in his mind.

It was answered in his mind.

"Boy! Gavin?"

"I'm here. Oh, Grandad!"

"Where . . . ? How . . . ? What's up, boy?"

"You . . . you . . ."

Bits of Gavin seemed to gather back into him, scraps of self flocking together, fitting themselves into place, the smell of hospital, a taste of salt like the sea, a round pale face floating in mist, huge round eyes—no human could really have eyes like that, or those whiskers. . . .

"You had a stroke, Grandad. It was really bad. You can't move, or talk, or anything. You're in hospital. I wanted to talk to you. You couldn't hear me. I asked the selkie to help, and she did it. I . . . I think I'm inside you. I'm really, really scared. I want to get out."

"Ah."

Grandad didn't say anything, but now that Gavin knew he was there, he could feel him pulling the bits of himself together too. More understandings came. The thuds were the sound of Grandad's heart, and the roaring was his blood moving round his body. And now he found he could remember the moments of sense and hold on to the knowledge that the someone had been Grandad all along, they'd been snatches of Grandad's own memories all muddled up with the bad-dream stuff. . . .

"You still there, boy? When . . . ?"

"It was twenty-seven days ago. We were up in your room. . . ."

Still in the same voiceless whisper Gavin started to tell him the story. He took it slowly. He could feel Grandad's tiredness, the effort of just listening, paying attention, of battling to hold on to himself as the roaring mist tried to rise. . . .

Now it surged up, unstoppable, like the tide in Stonehaven bay, flooding over the foreshore, covering rock and shingle and seaweed in the same shapeless sloshing mess of water,

101

sweeping Grandad away from him. But now that Gavin knew what was happening he found he could just about swim on that tide, just about keep his head above water, hold himself together while he called and called out in his mind, "Grandad! Grandad! I'm still here. Where are you?"

"Gavin? That you, boy? What's happened to me? What's going on, eh?"

"You've had a stroke, Grandad. You're in hospital. . . ."

Again he started the story, taking it slowly, giving Grandad time to rest, but again the mist returned and swept them apart. And again. And again, until Gavin learned to recognize the signs and stop telling the story and simply stay with Grandad in his mind, clinging to him in the roaring, thudding nowhere and whispering, "Hold on, Grandad. I'm here. It's going to be all right. Hold on."

Slowly, slowly, he thought he could feel Grandad getting stronger, keeping himself together more and more, beginning to answer Gavin's whispers. "In this together, eh? Good lad. We'll do. . . ."

It seemed to take forever, and now Gavin began to worry about what was happening *outside*, in the little ward where Grandad was lying on his bed and Gavin . . .

Where was Gavin, the real Gavin, the one with legs and arms and everything? How long had all this taken? Mum must be here by now; she'd have found him, if one of the nurses hadn't looked in sooner. He thought he could remember fainting, losing his balance, tumbling forward, clinging on to Grandad's hand to stop himself falling off the bed. . . . He must be lying across the bed. . . .

What would they do when they found him like that? They'd pick him up, and . . .

An appalling thought struck him.

Perhaps he wasn't still holding Grandad's hand! The nurses might have pulled them apart, so they could put Gavin on the other bed!

But that was how the selkie had got him into Grandad, through their hands!

Now he couldn't get back!

"Grandad! Am I still holding your hand?"

"Eh?"

"Your right hand! We were holding hands when the selkie put me here. That's how she did it. Through our hands. We mustn't let go. But the nurses are going to pull us apart when they find us. It's really important. I can't feel anything. Can you?"

"Hold it. . . . No. Doesn't seem to be working. Don't know where my hands are—or my feet, come to that."

"Let's see if we can do it together. I can sort of feel some of what you're feeling. Don says when you've had a stroke getting your body to do things is like trying to send messages somewhere they've had an earthquake, and all the telephone lines are down and the bridges are smashed and everything, and all you can do is keep sending messengers and perhaps one of them will get through. Come on, Grandad. Your right hand. Ready? Now . . ."

Where was his hand, his arm, his . . .

No, that wasn't any good. They were all *outside*. Where were Grandad's hand, arm, shoulder . . . ?

No good either, though he thought he could feel Grandad, somewhere close, trying. . . .

But there was nowhere to try, nowhere to begin, all melted away in the roaring mist. That isn't how your body works. Someone says, "Touch your nose," and your hand's there. Nothing about how you unconsciously summon arms, shoulders, all the different muscles. No, it was hopeless. . . .

*Oh, selkie . . . !*

Perhaps it was the thought of her—not the selkie who'd come to the ward just now, unless she was the same one that had popped her head out of the water when they'd been fishing down at the harbor almost a month ago—but for an instant he was back there, with Grandad beside him, fishing for mackerel. . . .

"Grandad!"

"Eh?"

"This is the wrong way. It's no use just telling your hand to do something. You've got to try and imagine it doing something—something it really knows how to do, something it does without you even thinking about it. What about a pendulum cast from the harbor wall? You remember when you were teaching me, showing me how. . . . Let's try and do that."

"Sorry, boy . . . no use . . . tired . . ."

He was, too. Gavin could feel his exhaustion, his hopelessness, but he had to go on.

"Please, Grandad! Listen. It's really important. If I let go of you I'll be stuck here, and I'll never get back. And someone's going to find us like this. Mum will be coming any moment, and she'll call the nurses and they'll make me let go so they can put me on the other bed, and I'll be here forever. Don't you see? Please, Grandad! I know you can do it. Just once. Please!"

No answer. The red mist roaring up, the thuds. Gavin fighting, forgetting everything except that he mustn't drown in the mist, melt away, be lost forever, but still in the dreary struggle whispering to Grandad, groping with fingers he didn't have for the touch of an imagined hand, and still holding it in his own as the mist faded and thinned . . . And then Grandad's whisper. A whisper weary beyond belief, with long pauses every few words. But still, somehow, changed.

"Sorry about that . . . Lost it for a bit. . . . Tired, boy . . . Got to get you out of here. . . . Casting a line worth a go . . . before I lose it again . . ."

"That's great, Grandad! We can do it. I know we can do it! What about that time I asked you how far you can send a line if you want to? And Tacky Steward was watching and he tried to beat you and got his line caught in a davit behind him."

Grandad actually chuckled at the memory.

"Tell me what you're doing, like you did then," Gavin suggested. "We're on the harbor wall. You've been teaching me. I got it right three times running. Tacky Steward's watching. Remember? Ready?

"How far can you cast if you really want to, Grandad?"

"Show you. Trick is, don't try too hard. Bit more line out, maybe—not too much. That'll do. Rod back, easy now—it's all in the rhythm. . . ."

Grandad had a beautiful cast. He seemed to do it absolutely without thinking—the rod angled back over his shoulder, the rod tip twitching to the movement of his hands, just enough to make the length of weighted line that hung from it start to swing like a pendulum, out, in, out, in, farther and farther each twitch until . . . He didn't need to look behind him, his hands knew by the feel of the rod the exact moment when the line had swung to the right point, and then *whoosh!* the rod sweeping forward, hurling the weight upward and outward so that it was moving far faster than the rod tip and then, as the rod slowed and stopped, the weight whistling on, pulling the line off the reel in a long, clean arc over the water, and finally falling with a little splash right out across the harbor.

There were angling societies that ran competitions how far people could cast. An expert with the right kit could do several hundred yards. Grandad could have done that too if he'd practiced, but he wasn't interested. He just wanted to catch fish.

Now, in his mind, Gavin whispered the words with him as he poured himself into the remembered moment, making it vivid, solid, seen and felt, the squeals of the gulls heard, the harbor smells in his nostrils, the faint salt taste of spray on his lips—and stronger, realer than any of those, the weight and feel of the rod in his hands, the twist of the right wrist that kept the line true as it went it whistling forward, *whoosh!* . . .

A jolt.

Darkness.

Falling.

Grandad's amazed whisper.

"Done it, boy! Got your hand!"

Voices—real voices, heard with real ears.

". . . found him like this. I think he's just fainted. He did it before, in casualty, when we first brought his grandfather in."

That was Mum. Then Véronique . . .

"Is all right, Mrs. Robinson. I just put him on the other bed, then I fetch Doctor."

*"Hold tight, Grandad! I've got to go! Hold tight!"*

*"Do my best."*

Mum again.

"Wait. They're holding hands. I'll just . . . No, I can't . . . They're too . . .You'll have to put him down. It isn't just Gavin holding on to Grandad. They're both doing it."

"But no—is not possible. Let me see. . . . Yes, you are right. Wait. I fetch Sister. . . ."

*"I've got to go now, Grandad. I think, if you help me . . . Can you still feel your arm?"*

*"Maybe. Something there."*

Yes, and now Gavin could feel it too, shadowy, uncertain but *something*, something really there in the utter nothingness. . . .

*"Just keep thinking about it, and I'll . . . Good-bye, Grandad. I'm going. . . ."*

*"Bye, boy . . ."*

And now Gavin was floating away through the darkness. Fainter and fainter came the roar of Grandad's blood, the slow thud of his heart. It was like being swept along a pitch-black tunnel, where he could almost sense the walls brushing close by, and kept trying to duck because he was about to bash into something solid in the darkness ahead. . . . Mum's voice.

"No! Please leave him! Something's happening! He's moving! Just leave him! You don't know what you're doing!"

(Good old Mum!)

And then, sudden and shocking as the lights being switched on in the tunnel, pain.

Pain in his right hand, his own hand, real. Grandad's strong, workman's grip, almost crushing his fingers.

And then all of himself, all the real Gavin, with the hummock of Grandad's body beneath his own chest, the feel of bedclothes against his own left cheek, his own legs dangling down to the floor, their two hands still clasped tight, Mum holding his own other hand, her voice in his own ears . . .

"Gavin. Gavin. Are you all right, darling? Take it easy. . . ."

"I'm all right," he croaked. "Just . . . Wait."

He pulled his hand out of hers and eased himself half up. Propping himself on the bed, he staggered along beside it until he was leaning over Grandad's pillow.

"It's all right, Grandad," he gasped. "I'm out. I'm standing by your bed. You can let go now."

Grandad made a grunting sound. Slowly the iron grip eased, the fingers straightened. But the room seemed to be getting darker. The bed was swaying about. Someone—Véronique?—was saying something. She sounded surprised.

Not enough. He needed a clear signal. Something Lena could tell the consultant.

"Grandad! Don't go away! I'm here. Now . . . Ready? Touch your nose."

A pause. A tiny spasm. Jerkily, with huge effort, Grandad's

forearm rose from the bedclothes, hovered while the trembling fingers straightened, and his hand lowered itself to fumble around his face, find his mustache, and settle onto his nose. Below his strange, clipped mustache his lips twitched.

This time Gavin fainted for real.

# 12

When Gavin unfainted he knew exactly what was going on. He couldn't have been out long. He was still in the ward. They'd just put him on the other bed and covered him up with something. Véronique was explaining to someone, Sister, probably, what had happened. He kept his eyes shut because he wasn't going to tell anyone about the selkie, or being inside Grandad, and he needed to listen so that he could think what to say.

". . . is no doubt. It is not Gavin holding. Mr. Robinson is holding Gavin's hand. The grip is strong. With one hand I cannot break it. Then I fetch you and you see how Gavin tells him, Let go, and he lets go. He tells him, Touch your nose. He does it."

"That's right," said Mum. "Gavin had obviously got through to his grandfather somehow, but the whole thing's been an appalling strain for him, he's been putting so much into it—we've been seriously worried how hard he was taking it—and it was too much for him when it suddenly happened, and he passed out."

At that point Gavin opened his eyes and muttered, "Where am I? What's happening?" the way you're supposed to.

"Darling!" said Mum. "It's all right. No, don't try and get up. You're in Grandad's ward. You just fainted, like you did last time. You'll be all right in a moment."

"I talked to Grandad," he muttered.

"Yes, I know. We saw you. That's wonderful. It's amazing. How did you do it?"

He let his voice grow a bit stronger.

"I don't know. I was just talking to him—about fishing down at the harbor—casting—and I was holding his hand—felt it sort of move—as if he was thinking about casting, you know—so I sort of guessed—he could hear me—told him to hold my hand, and—and . . ."

He closed his eyes and lay back. It was only half fake—he felt tireder than he'd ever felt in his life, but happy with it, amazingly, extraordinarily happy. With the selkie's help he'd got through! He'd talked to Grandad! If he'd had any strength at all he'd have wanted to dance and sing.

"Take it easy, darling. Don't try and do anything. You can stay here as long as you like."

"Doctor'll be wanting to keep him in for observation, most likely," said Sister.

"No! Mum, please . . ."

He started to push himself up, but collapsed. Mum was great.

"Take it easy," she said. "Of course you can go home if you want to. You just need a bit of a rest."

"I think, perhaps, Mrs. Robinson, when the doctor—"

"Of course, if there's a good medical reason why he should stay in I won't object, provided that nothing's done to him without my express permission. But if it's only another faint he'll be much better off where he wants to be. I'll talk to the doctor."

(Good old Mum! Getting it right. Knowing just what to do and say when it mattered. Like not letting them pull his hand away from Grandad's before he was safely out. As soon as he got her alone he was going to give her a really juicy hug.)

"I'm all right," he said firmly. "I really am. It's my fault. I didn't have any lunch."

"Well, that wasn't very bright of you," said Mum, relaxing. "I'll just see he has something in his stomach before I take him home, Sister, and then he'll be fine, don't you think? I'd like to be off as soon as we can manage, so I can tell my mother-in-law the news. . . ."

It was still, clear evening as they drove back to Stonehaven, all gold and pink in the sunset. It was as if the whole world felt the way Gavin felt, just like it had on the filthy wet evening when they'd brought Grandad to the hospital and Gavin had dropped the pizza. Things were going to be all right.

He wasn't going to tell anyone what had happened—if it *had* happened. There were two ways of looking at it. Either it could have been a dream—he'd been starting to faint and he'd hallucinated the selkie and everything else just at the moment when Grandad had broken through whatever had been holding him back—maybe it had been Gavin suddenly thumping down across his body that had made that happen. Could be.

Or else the selkie had been real, and somehow he and Grandad had got involved with her, giving her the mackerel and talking to her the way he had, and then again just before Grandad had had his stroke. He didn't think she'd caused the stroke—she was touchy, maybe, and mischievous, but she wasn't that mean. Or that powerful. She couldn't change stuff in the real, bricks-and-concrete world. What she could do was change stuff in your mind if she could get through to you, change how you saw and felt things—"cast a glamour," they call it in the fantasy games.

The stroke had been due to happen anyway, Donald had said. And it had happened just as Grandad and Gavin had somehow got her attention—summoned her, sort of—by talking about the selkies. So now she was involved, but there wasn't any way she could help Grandad, not directly. All she could do was help Gavin, get him somewhere where she could cast a glamour on him, change him, so that he could get through to Grandad. She'd given him a bit of a nudge every time he'd sort-of summoned her again by talking to Grandad about the selkies. But that still hadn't been enough. He'd still been too much tied in to the real world, hospitals and meals and school and all that. She'd needed him looser, freer . . . crazier.

Crazy enough to think it might make a difference if he gave her *Selkie*.

Loose enough to get out of his own body and into Grandad.

Well, maybe. He wouldn't ever know, not for sure. Anyway, it'd be much easier if everyone else thought he'd just fainted from lack of food and the shock of Grandad grabbing on to his hand. It didn't matter what had really happened. He could just go on privately believing that maybe it had been the selkie who'd done it, and not having to argue about it and everyone humoring him and saying inside themselves, Poor Gavin, no wonder he's a wee bit crazy after what he's been through.

He wasn't, not any longer. In fact he felt that the selkie—if there was a selkie—had maybe done something for him, just as she had for Grandad. He'd learned stuff, started to understand stuff, during that awful time inside Grandad, feeling how he felt, remembering bits and pieces out of his long life—stuff about time, and living through it, and growing older, and, in the end, dying. Of course he'd known all along that that's what happens to people, but he'd never really felt it, understood about it, believed deep down it was going to happen to anyone he cared about, even old Dodgem. He did now.

So things were going to be all right. They weren't going to be fairy-tale all right—that doesn't happen—but Grandad was going to be Grandad again, however ill he was, there, inside his body, knowing what was happening, even if he could only mumble about it. He might get almost completely well in the end. Probably it would be less than that. But with luck one sunny morning next spring Gavin was going to take him down to the harbor in his wheelchair, and they'd settle into their usual spot on the harbor wall, and Gavin would take Grandad's light rod and cast a line for him, and put the rod into his hands, and they'd fish for mackerel together. That would still be pretty good, after everything that had happened. Perhaps it would be even less than that, and Grandad would never get out of his bed again, and then after a few more months he would slip quietly away into death. But Gavin would still have something. He would have been able, before that, to hold Grandad's hand and know that Grandad could hear him and understand, even if he could only mumble in answer, so that when the time came they could say good-bye. Gavin would miss him dreadfully, and be miserable for a long time after. But in the end it would be all right, because he would still have

Grandad sort of inside him, a presence, a memory he could always go back to, whenever he needed.

But suppose he hadn't got through. Suppose Grandad had stayed sleeping, deep in his endless nightmare, and then died still not understanding what had happened to him. In that case all Gavin would have had was a loss, a dark, cold hole inside himself, that nothing would ever fill or heal for the rest of his days. Thanks to the selkie, it wasn't going to be like that now.

They got home almost an hour earlier than usual.

"How are you feeling, darling?" said Mum as they got out of the car. "Do you want to go and lie down for a bit?"

"I'm fine, Mum. I really am. I feel great. I want to dance and sing. No I don't—I want to get myself really hungry for supper, so what I'll do is take Dodgem down to the beach."

"Oh, darling! Don't you think—"

"Please, Mum. You go in and tell Gran, so she can ring up all her friends. Look, I'll take my mobile, and if I feel tired I'll call you and you can come and pick us up. I promise. Please!"

He flung his arms round her and gave her her hug. She hugged him back, and then took him by the arms and looked at him, smiling. He was a bit surprised to realize that he'd really meant that hug, and that actually he was very fond of her. It isn't the sort of thing you often think about, but she'd been wonderful all along, letting him get on with his craziness, though she must have been worried sick about it, just that once telling him he couldn't go to the hospital every day—and she'd been dead right about that too—knowing he'd had to work it through for himself, not nagging him at all.

"You're a funny boy," she said. "After all these years I still don't really know where I am with you. Oh, all right. Off you go. Don't be more than an hour."

"Can you send out for a pizza, please? The one with the anchovies?"

"I'd better get the big one."


The tide was about halfway in, with a big moon just rising. He left Dodgem nosing into sea wrack and crunched down across the shingle and the gritty, shell-strewn sand until he reached the gently lapping waves. For a while he simply stood there gazing at the moon, not thinking but feeling, letting his sense of relief and thankfulness and happiness flood up through him and fill him to the brim. The evening breeze, from the cooler sea onto the sun-warmed land, blew gently in his face.

Without thinking about it he knew he was on the edge of things, between sea and shore, between night and day, between Grandad's life and Grandad's death, between his own world and the selkie's. This was the right moment, the right place. They would never come again.

He raised his hands and spread them in front of him.

"Thank you," he whispered. "Thank you very much."

He waited a long while, hoping the selkie would appear, but knowing she almost certainly wouldn't. He just needed something more, he didn't know what, but something to tell him it was truly over. Nothing happened. He'd said he'd be back in an hour. With a sigh he turned away and started up the beach. Ahead of him Dodgem lifted his nose out of a mess of sea wrack and stood staring out to sea with strips of seaweed dangling either side of his muzzle. He barked. He was pretty well blind to anything more than a few yards off, but automatically Gavin turned to see what he was looking at.

Now, from this slightly higher viewpoint, though it had hardly begun to get dark, he could see the pale moon-path across the ripples. There was something there, right in the middle of it. The selkie, after all? No, that wasn't how seals moved, and it was too far out of the water.

Next moment he knew what it was.

He turned and walked a few paces farther up the shore to a dry rock, where he sat down and took off his shoes and socks. He went back and waded into the water.

The breeze brought *Selkie* smoothly to him, sailing like a dream.

# AUTHOR'S NOTE

The big hospital in Aberdeen is called the Royal Aberdeen Hospital, but they're busy people at the RAH and I didn't like to bother them with a mass of questions about exactly how they do things there, so I've made that part up and changed the name. Even so, there was a lot of medical stuff I didn't know and couldn't find in books, so I'm enormously grateful to Lucy Curtice for helping me out with that.

Otherwise everything in and around Stonehaven is as real as I could make it. Two of my grandsons live there, and they're sure to let me know if I've got anything wrong.

## ABOUT THE AUTHOR

PETER DICKINSON is the author of many books for adults and young readers and has won numerous awards, including the Carnegie Medal (twice), the *Guardian* Award, and the Whitbread Award (also twice). His novel *Eva* was a *Boston Globe–Horn Book* Fiction Honor Book. *Eva* was also selected as an ALA Best Book for Young Adults, as were his novels *AK* and *A Bone from a Dry Sea*. *The Lion Tamer's Daughter and Other Stories* was chosen as a Best Book of the Year by *School Library Journal*. *The Ropemaker* was selected as a Michael L. Printz Honor Book for Young Adults by the American Library Association. His most recent book was *The Tears of the Salamander*. He has four grown children and lives in Hampshire, England, with his wife, the writer Robin McKinley.